*He wanted to kiss those lips. He wanted to taste her, to please her.*

His eyes lifted to her full, red mouth, parted with anticipation, with invitation. The bright color contrasted with her pale skin as perfectly as did her dark, full lashes. He wanted to tell her everything he longed to do to her, intended to do to her. But something in her eyes kept him from speaking. She was…insecure. Nervous. He didn't remember the last time he'd seen such things in a woman. Had he ever? Those things touched him deeply, aroused him profoundly.

Instinct told him he had a choice to make. He could wait and allow her to act—but did he dare risk her running away? Perhaps he should press forward, take what he wanted—take his pleasure and take her passion—then take her on a ride to satisfaction she would never forget.

Dear Reader,

Coming up with a sexy holiday story is always a lot of fun, and I actually had the pleasure of writing this one during the month of December, surrounded by a winter's snow. Having moved to New York from Texas last year, I've learned that snow can be quite romantic! Lots of reasons to snuggle! And who doesn't enjoy a little sexy romance this time of year? Whip out the mistletoe and let the sexy fun begin. Caron Avery certainly finds some when a charity auction mix-up has her Dressed to Thrill in a Marilyn Monroe costume. Suddenly, conservative little Caron is a bombshell with a hot man at her side.

I loved writing Caron because she is such a real person, full of flaws, insecurities, dreams and desires. The costume allows her to set those things aside, to feel she is Cinderella for a night. The most engaging part of Caron and her costume, though, is not how she reacts to wearing it, but how she reacts to her man when she no longer has it as her guide.

Let the romance begin!

Happy Holidays, everyone!

Lisa Renee Jones

# Lisa Renee Jones

## SANTA, BABY

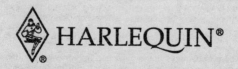

HARLEQUIN®

TORONTO • NEW YORK • LONDON
AMSTERDAM • PARIS • SYDNEY • HAMBURG
STOCKHOLM • ATHENS • TOKYO • MILAN • MADRID
PRAGUE • WARSAW • BUDAPEST • AUCKLAND

Recycling programs
for this product may
not exist in your area.

ISBN-13: 978-0-373-79514-7

SANTA, BABY

www.eHarlequin.com

**Printed in U.S.A.**

# ABOUT THE AUTHOR

Lisa lives in New York, where she spends her days writing the dreams playing in her head. Before becoming a writer, Lisa lived the life of a corporate executive, often taking the red-eye flight out of town and flying home for the excitement of a Little League baseball game. Visit Lisa at Lisareneejones.com

## Books by Lisa Renee Jones

HARLEQUIN BLAZE
339—HARD AND FAST
442—LONE STAR SURRENDER

HARLEQUIN NOCTURNE
THE BEAST WITHIN
BEAST OF DESIRE
BEAST OF DARKNESS

Thanks to Samantha Hunter, Karen Foley, and Tawny Weber, for being my partners in the Dressed to Thrill miniseries. You ladies rock! It's been an honor. And thanks to the editors at Blaze for bringing us together and making this possible. As always, love and appreciation to my family. Lastly—thank you to Janice for helping me make this, and so many books, possible!

# *Prologue*

THE MONDAY AFTER THANKSGIVING, Josie spent at the costume rental shop, Dressed to Thrill, where she worked, putting together the costumes for a big San Francisco charity event. "Starlets of Hollywood" was the theme for the party, but before sending it out, she was claiming the Marilyn Monroe costume as her own. For a night. This night. After all, the iconic white dress didn't have to be shipped for two more days, and she needed this costume to make *her* fantasies come true. To heck with everyone else and their thrills. It was time for *hers*.

Her flirtation with Tom, the delivery guy, had to come to some conclusion. Enough with the flirtation that had gone on for months. No more flashing her with sexy smiles and lusty, blue-eyed stares without action to back them up. Her poor body could not take any more of this wanting and needing…and wanting. It was time to get serious and either make this thing with Tom happen, or move on.

She glanced at the clock. Near noon. She'd called Tom's employer and asked to have her delivery person call hours ago. Any minute now, her boss, Carol, would arrive, and Carol didn't like flirtation on the job. She'd caught Tom and Josie in the act once, and it had not been pleasant.

She tapped her pink-painted nails on the counter, willing Tom to call, and then busied herself folding the Audrey Hepburn costume for the charity event. Good grief, she thought, studying the simple, conservative sheath dress. It was barely what Josie would call a costume. Certainly not a fantasy waiting to happen. More a boring night to be endured.

The phone jingled and Josie jumped, her heart racing. It was him, it was Tom. She just knew it. She pressed her fist to her chest, willing herself to calm, and answered. "Dressed to Thrill."

"Josie," came the sexy male voice she'd come to lust after all too often.

"Hi, Tom. Thanks for calling."

"You have some sort of special delivery you needed me for?"

"Yes, actually," she said, swiping at her own blond bangs nervously. "The delivery is for you."

"No problem. I'll pick it up. Any special instructions?"

"Yes," she said. "I mean—the delivery is for you, Tom. I need you to come after the store closes. Once you're off work."

Silence. She could hear her heart thrumming in her ears. Was he going to say no? Was he going to turn her down? How would she face him later if he did? Then, "Eight o'clock good for you, Josie?"

She smiled. "Eight is perfect."

"Looking forward to it, Josie." And then he hung up.

DRESSED IN THE SLEEK, low-cut Marilyn dress with cleavage that would set any man on fire, Josie was ready and waiting. And hotter than she had imagined possible. The white dress, the wig, the red-painted lips. She barely recognized herself. The wig, she decided, was the final touch. Sure, she was blonde already, but there was something about that wig—a certain seductive quality that it added.

The doorbell sounded at the front door, which was locked to allow Josie warning of Tom's arrival. Besides. She didn't want anyone but Tom inside this fantasy tonight.

And he was here. This was it. The moment of truth. Her stomach fluttered wildly, and Josie rushed forward, a bit wobbly on her heels, which she blamed on nerves. She rounded the corner and slowed to a sexy sashay as she approached the door and unlocked it. She opened the door and stuck a hip out, hand resting there. "Hiya Tom."

His deep blue eyes swept her seductive dress and lingered on her deep cleavage, sending a shiver of delight up her spine. "You never cease to amaze me, Josie."

"You like the dress?"

"I like the woman."

She swallowed hard, aching in all the intimate places that the dress barely covered. "Come inside," she said, appalled when her voice cracked, and thankful for the chance to recover a bit, as she eased out of his way to allow his entry.

He stepped across the foyer, still dressed in his brown uniform and she didn't mind one bit. She loved the nice way it hugged his tight bum and stretched across impressive shoulders. The instant he was inside, she shut the door and locked it. She turned to face him, stared up into those clear blue eyes and went blank.

Completely, utterly blank. Josie could not remember what she'd planned next.

"Josie?" he asked softly.

She wet her lips. Inwardly, she shook herself. Don't blow this!

"This way," she said and started forward—slowly so she could work the sexy strut that her heels and dress allowed, enjoying the swish of the silky material around her legs and leading Tom to a private dressing room she had set up with candles and dinner.

Entering the room, she motioned to the table she had set up. "I hope you like Chinese. Or I know you do. You told me. One day. When you were here." Shut up! She tried to look sexy again—did the hand-on-hip thing. It seemed to give her something to do with her hands. She sure wished he would.

Tom stared at her, blue eyes getting darker by the minute. Hungry, but not for food. She inhaled and decided to be bold. "Or we could just move to dessert."

She barely blinked and he was in front of her, those hard-earned muscles from his delivery work flexing with delicious force as he pulled her close, wrapping those wonderful arms around her.

"I like *you*, Josie," he said. "I like everything about you."

"You do?" she said, warmth spreading through her limbs. "I mean I thought you did, but you never acted on it." Her fingers splayed over that deliciously broad chest. "Why didn't you do something about it?"

"Because every day since your boss caught us flirting, she's given me dirty looks. I didn't want to get you in trouble."

She could live with that answer. Definitely. "Go ahead," she encouraged. "Get me in trouble."

"On one condition," he said, his breath feathering her with warm temptation, the promise of a long-awaited kiss.

"What's that?" she asked breathlessly.

"I love the costumes, Josie," he said, referring to the many she'd shown him these past few months, trying to impress him. "But once I undress Marilyn," he said, "send the costume to a customer and let me have the real woman from now on."

Could he have said anything better? She smiled, ready for that "action" she'd been longing for. "Undress me, baby," she teased. The charity ball could have their Marilyn. She would happily be simply herself. Because Marilyn might have given her the courage to invite Tom to dinner, but *Josie* had gotten her man.

# 1

*SHE WOKE FROM restless slumber, warm with aware-*
*ness, sensing that she was not alone, sensing that*
*he was there, that he had once again come to her.*
*Anticipation thrummed through her limbs, and she*
*pushed herself to a sitting position, leaning against*
*the padded headboard behind her, eyes drawn to*
*the balcony, to the billowing curtains dancing in*
*the midnight air. Hungrily, her gaze lingered there,*
*riveted to the shadows beyond the white lace*
*fabric, her thighs pressed together against the*
*heated desire burning a path up their length.*

*Movement scattered the shadows, sent her*
*heart racing. Her breath lodged in her throat as*
*he stepped forward, his fair hair lifting with the*
*wind and falling around broad, leather-clad*
*shoulders. Crystal blue eyes touched hers, eyes so*
*deeply colored, they reached across the small*
*space and swept her into their scorching depths.*
*In the distance, a drum played.*

No. She frowned. Not a drum. A knock. A knock on
the door.

Oh! Caron Avery snapped back to the present, her

gaze shifting from the romance novel in her hand to her office door inside the Book Nook, her San Francisco bookstore. She'd used her savings and a loan from her grandmother to purchase the bookstore two years before. A daring move she still couldn't believe she'd made.

Another knock sounded at the door. "Just a minute!" she called, opening a desk drawer and shoving the book inside, next to the tropical cruise brochure she'd been fantasizing over for her upcoming thirtieth birthday. She slammed the drawer shut, telling herself she had nothing to hide. She was just doing research; learning about the product offerings of her store.

After all, her recent decision to take her eccentric little store in a more distinctive direction and begin catering to women's fiction, had paid off big-time. Sales had ramped up in a major way. She'd even managed to hire some staff. Well, one person. But that was better than being on her own. Soon, the whole upstairs of the store would be converted entirely to women's interests, filled with books, candles and gifts—a special place for women to privately explore their hearts' desires, from inspirational reads to sizzling red-hot page-turners. A successful decision, indeed.

So much so, that she had almost paid her grandmother back every dime she'd borrowed. Even sooner as Christmas was only a few weeks away, and sales were booming. An amazingly wonderful feeling considering a plane crash had stolen her parents from her at age five. But her grandmother had always been there for her, no questions asked—quickly offering her the cash to chase her dream.

Caron tucked a wisp of unruly brunette hair back

into the confines of her neatly groomed bun and squeezed her thighs together, feeling the lingering fire of her fantasy taunting her. No doubt, her lack of a social life was catching up to her.

"Come in!" she called, lacing her fingers together on the desk and returning to her prim and proper librarian persona. The one that was real, not fantasy. The one she wished she had the courage to discard, but feared she never would.

The door swung open and her assistant manager, Kasey Washington, darted into the office, excitement lighting her youthful features, her cute little blond bob bouncing as she rushed toward the desk.

"Oh, my gosh!" Kasey exclaimed. "I have big, big news." She plopped down in the worn, cloth-covered chair Caron had bought at a secondhand store. "Big news!" Caron pursed her lips. To Kasey, a new flavor at Starbucks constituted big news. Kasey grinned and continued, "One of our new romance customers is upstairs looking around. I don't know if you remember her? Ruth Parker."

Caron shook her head. "Doesn't sound familiar."

"She said you helped her pick out a couple of books last week and she really liked you."

*Okay.* "That's great to hear," Caron said, and silently added, *But hardly big, big news!*

"She works for the Cancer Society, and she's on the committee that is sponsoring that big charity event going on a week from Friday, the old Hollywood-style Gala they've been advertising for weeks. Well—" her eyes lit "—one of the ladies in the runway show had an emergency and can't make it. She needs someone to play Audrey Hepburn and she wants you!" She squealed. "How cool is that? You're going to be on television."

Caron's jaw dropped. "What?" She shook her head. "Oh, no. I'm not getting up in front of all those people dressed in a costume. And I am not going on television!"

"You have to!" Kasey insisted. "It's fun. It's exciting. It's a once in a lifetime opportunity. You said you wanted to do something out of the ordinary, to cut loose a little."

Caron didn't do public speaking, let alone walk across a stage in front of a bunch of society people *and* on television. "By taking a cruise! Not going on television. No. This is not fun to me."

"The store will be in television commercials, in every brochure handed out and in publicity after the event. And for free. She isn't even asking for a donation because the spot is paid for already. This is free publicity for the store and perfect to launch our new romance section and it's the first Friday of December, right smack in the midst of holiday shopping. Talk about a last-minute chance to boost Christmas sales. It's perfect! Go be Audrey for a night. Have fun." She wiggled an eyebrow. "There will be lots of hot, rich men there. In fact, now that I think about it, you have to take me. *We* have to do this. You have to do it. For the store, Caron. Do it for the store. You know we need the exposure. It could mean lots of business."

Leaning back in her chair, Caron scowled at her assistant. Because Kasey was right. They needed the exposure. And exposure equaled business, which equaled paying her grandmother back the rest of the money she owed her. Suddenly, this wasn't about stepping outside her comfort zone and doing something that felt awkward. This was about responsibility and what was right.

"She's here now?" Caron asked. "Waiting to talk with me?"

"Right outside the door," Kasey agreed. "Your ticket to adventure and great sales. I can feel it."

Caron rolled her chair back from her desk. "I can't believe I am going to do this," she murmured.

Kasey hopped to her feet. "Yes! This is going to be so much fun. Just wait and see. You are going to have a blast. A night of pure fantasy. Did I mention you get a celebrity stylist and hours of being pampered before the show? You are going to be in heaven. You are going to be Audrey Hepburn for a night. To live a fantasy. I'm so excited for you, but jealous. Really jealous."

Right. Fantasy. Audrey Hepburn. Maybe that might be okay. If she could forget the crowds. Right. Forget. The. Crowds. Forget falling down on stage during her high school graduation. She'd never quite gotten over that, but she'd better get over it now. Audrey Hepburn wouldn't fall down, after all. And they wanted *her*— Caron Avery—to be Audrey for a night.

FRIDAY NIGHT CAME far too quickly, especially in the midst of a busy work schedule that did nothing to abate her nerves. At five o'clock, Caron had been headed toward the Gala for professional primping done by experts, when she'd received the news—the toilet had overflowed in the bookstore. Immediately detouring, she'd rushed back to the store, unable to leave Kasey to such ugliness on her own. An argument with the plumber had ensued over his outrageous fees, and she'd fired him in favor of someone she could afford to pay. The result—toilet fixed but she was late for her appointment with makeup and hair. Almost two hours late. Terribly, horribly late. And since there was absolutely no parking to be found in the hotel parking garage, any relief she had found in finally arriving at the five-star downtown Hyatt was quickly fading. Could this get any more embarrassing?

Caron's little red Volkswagen sputtered on the third go-round in the parking lot, and one look at the gas gauge said, yes, it could get worse. Her car was on empty. She blew strands of dark hair from her eyes. This was not exactly the making of a Cinderella fantasy night.

Desperate times required desperate measures. She lightly pedaled the accelerator, ever aware of her fuel gauge, and turned toward the front door of the hotel. Mini Christmas trees flickering with white lights lined the entryway, and she pulled up behind a line of cars waiting for the valet. Wow! Already people in fancy dresses and tuxes were speckled along the sidewalk and entryway. This was beyond late. This was downright cringe-worthy.

Desperate times, she reminded herself. She shifted into Park and killed the engine. She slid out of the car despite being more than a little self-conscious about her pink sweatpants and butterfly-print T-shirt. Her face was bare of makeup, her hair piled on top of her head. A wilted flower amongst the glamorous roses in glittery dresses. Nevertheless, the fastest path to the entrance, and the parking of her car, was right there, in front of her. She slammed the car door shut and tried to think of the bright side. Instead, she thought how little time the stylist had to transform her into runway-ready. At least she didn't have time for nerves. There was a light at the end of the long, twisting, black tunnel called this day.

Spotting a doorman, she rushed forward, ignoring the horns honking as several cars pulled forward and her Volkswagen remained in place. She half ran to the uniformed attendant, hoping to reach him ahead of a lady in an elegant white formal suit. She hated to be rude, but she had to get into that hotel.

Caron held out her keys, panting a bit breathlessly. "I'm in the show, and I'm very, very late." A gorgeous brunette in a red satin gown walked by, and Caron cringed, her pink sweats feeling dingier by the minute. "Make that three verys. I have to get into costume and I can't find a parking spot and—"

"Miss. I have cars ahead of you. I can't just move you ahead."

This was the part where she needed money that she didn't have. The part where someone rich hands cash to the naysayer and makes them a yeah-sayer. Sometimes she really hated the way money made the world go round.

She plunged onward in her argument. "Again," she said. "I'm in the show. I'm one of the Hollywood starlets—Audrey Hepburn. They can't start without me." He gave her a quick inspection that said he'd believe that the day hell froze over. She frowned. "I'm aware I don't look the role at the moment. I missed my appointment with hair and makeup. The toilet at my store…"

He snatched her keys. "I'll take care of it," he said grudgingly.

Apparently, the mention of a toilet was almost as good as cash. It sure scored her a parking spot. Whatever worked. Now if she could get a ticket to claim her car and disappear. And she almost wished she could just disappear. Unfortunately, it looked as if she'd need that cruise to get her fantasy escape. Tonight was turning into one big flop.

On that note, she accepted the ticket from the valet and whirled toward the door and right into the hard, tuxedo-clad chest of a man. His hands came out to steady her—strong hands—warm hands that sent a shock wave of awareness through her body.

She blinked up into the amber gaze of a handsome face framed with dark hair, a hint of gray sprinkled at the temples. Very George Clooney—Ocean's Thirteen sexy with a strong, square jaw, and firm, nice lips. Oh, God. Don't look at his lips. Back to those amber eyes. Eyes that inspected her pink butterfly shirt with a lifted eyebrow. She swallowed. She'd made it to the fantasy but managed to do it in pink sweats and tennis shoes.

This was so *her* life, not Cinderella's.

SHE HAD BLUE EYES. That was the first thought that came to his mind as he stared down at the heart-shaped face of the woman who'd unwittingly become his prey. Sky-blue, deep, almost navy with a hint of yellow. He'd guessed green from a distance, a contrast to her dark brown hair. But he liked the blue. He hadn't been on the hunt in a long time; and on this night, certainly, he hadn't expected to be. But there was no denying the demand within him for this woman—the primal hunger she'd taken from dormant to downright raging. The minute he'd seen the pink sweat suit in the midst of the clingy silk gowns, he'd stood at attention.

"I am so sorry." The woman apologized for running into him, her voice as adorable as her pointed chin and cute button nose. "I am sort of in a rush. The makeup people are going to kill me. I…sorry."

"I'm not," he replied, reluctantly letting go of her petite shoulders when everything male inside him roared with demand. A demand to pull her close. No. He wasn't sorry at all. In fact, he'd put himself in her path for a reason. To meet her. "I'm Baxter Remington. You are?"

She swallowed hard. She had a slender neck, a neck meant for kissing. "Baxter Remington," she repeated. "As in the Baxter Remington who owns Remington's? With coffee bars all over the United States?"

And Canada, but he didn't say that. It still amazed him that his father's little dream was launching into a global enterprise. "You know our coffee?"

"Of course," she said. "The shops are everywhere." She crinkled her nose. "It's a little pricey for me, though." Her eyes flared, as if she realized she'd misspoken. She quickly added, "But worth it. I just can't afford…I mean…" She obviously cringed. "I'm late. I need to go. Sorry again." She started to leave.

"Wait!" he called out before he could stop himself.

"Sir?" The valet was standing beside Baxter, offering service for Baxter's 911 Porsche sitting a few steps from the curb.

Baxter held up an impatient hand and focused on the female turning back to him with surprise on her face, as if she hadn't expected him to continue their conversation. Certainly, she hadn't lured him to call after her as most of the women he knew would. Was that what intrigued him? Her unassuming nature? And yet she sent fire through his veins. She wasn't his normal blonde, blue-eyed, big-breasted, thirty-second distraction, then back to work. She was brunette, and wore no makeup. There were no plastic bells and whistles, either, just pure, natural woman. Pretty, earthy, genuine.

"How do I find you later?" he asked.

Her lips parted in hesitation, and then a slow smile lit her features. "Look for Audrey Hepburn." And then she turned and rushed away.

Baxter stared after her; the thrum of carnal desire burned through his body. To think he'd almost skipped this event, since there was more than coffee brewing right now at Remington. He was hot in the midst of allegations about his VP's supposed insider trading, which he hoped like hell weren't true. A good reason to hide from the press. Seems little Miss Audrey Hepburn had given him a reason to come out and play.

# 2

CARON WAS STILL REELING from her encounter with the ultrasexy Baxter Remington when she hit the backstage area of the show. All around her women were fretting in front of mirrors, while stylists attended to last-minute touch-ups to hair and makeup. The nervous energy in the room was so darn electric, it was contagious. It rushed over Caron and set alight the idea of embracing her persona as Audrey Hepburn for the night.

Her mind raced as she searched for the lead stylist, Betsy, to announce her arrival. Illicit thoughts of living out a fantasy—with Baxter Remington in the starring male role, and she, the sophisticated starlet—took root. She almost laughed at that. She'd met the man in a sweat suit, with no makeup on—a guise that wasn't uncommon on her days off. It was comfortable. And men like Baxter Remington did not *do* women like her. Not that she wanted to do him. Or him to do her, rather. She grimaced. Okay. Maybe she did. If she was going to live a fantasy, why not *do* a man as hot as Baxter? That highly sensual, quite entertaining idea lasted all of two seconds before being smashed nice and flat as she found Betsy.

"I'm here," she announced, and smiled nervously. "Just in time, right?"

"We already replaced you." Betsy delivered the message with all the brassy personality that her red hair and bodacious curves suggested. Did so while still managing to stick some bobby pins in the wig of what appeared to be a business owner representing Elizabeth Taylor.

Disappointment washed over Caron, and she whispered, "Replaced me?"

"What'd you expect me to do, sugar?" Betsy challenged. A hand went to her robust hip. "You're hours late. Not one hour. *Hours late.* As in plural." She raked fingers through a mess of wild red curls. "I had to turn one of the makeup girls into Audrey, and that wasn't an easy task." She grimaced. "Suzie barely fit her size-eight body into your size-four dress. I worked miracles, I tell you. Miracles."

"I really loved that dress," Caron half whispered to herself.

"*You* weren't here," Betsy countered.

"I know," Caron admitted, feeling the heat of embarrassment and disappointment rush to her cheeks. "I left a message. I had a plumbing problem."

"And I was in poo up to my neck," Betsy spat. "This event is televised, and my job is to fill these dresses with starlet look-alikes before those cameras roll." She motioned to all the craziness around her. "And do I look like I could check messages? I have a show to put on."

"And a problem to solve," came a male voice.

Caron, Betsy and Elizabeth Taylor all turned to find Reginald, Betsy's assistant, holding a blond wig. Betsy grabbed Elizabeth Taylor's shoulder, and Elizabeth yelped. Betsy quickly apologized, dropping her hand but not the grimace on her face.

"Why are you holding Marilyn's hair?" she asked, her face redder than Caron's felt.

Reginald was a tall, black, effeminate man, with better grooming than a lot of the women she knew. "Because," he said, lips pursed, "*Marilyn* doesn't like high heels and never wears them, thus, how she fell down the stairs and broke her ankle. She's out. No show for her."

"Come again?" Betsy asked, blinking as if she didn't believe what she'd heard.

"She's out, Betsy. We lost our star!" Reginald was losing his cool.

Betsy turned slowly, and fixed her attention on Caron. "You'll be Marilyn."

Caron's eyes went wide. "Are you nuts? I don't look anything like Marilyn."

"The dress will swallow her whole," Reginald interjected.

"Turn Suzie into Marilyn," Caron suggested. "Let me have my Audrey dress back."

"Listen," Betsy commanded, "I sewed her into that thing. She's not coming out anytime soon. You're Marilyn, honey. You owe me for being so late." She waved at Reginald. "Get the dress, and let me work my miracles."

Caron looked down at her B-cup chest. "I don't have the equipment."

"It's time for you to learn the miracles of the push-up, gel bra. You'll never again leave home without one."

Reginald reappeared with a figure-hugging white

dress, and Caron's mouth went dry. "Are we doing this?" he asked.

"I need you, Caron," Betsy said.

It had taken her all week to embrace her walk down the runway as the demure, sophisticated Audrey Hepburn. She had all of thirty seconds to decide on a very different role—the sexy, sensational Marilyn Monroe. Did she dare? Caron inhaled, thinking of paying back her grandmother, of the exposure this event would deliver to her store and her future. And yes, the adventure she'd been craving came to mind, as well. Responsibility and adventure—an enticing combination. She made her decision. Yes—she dared.

FBI AGENT SARAH WALKER slid a hand over her silver satin-covered hip and sashayed into action, speaking low into her invisible mike. "I have Baxter Remington in view. Repeat, target in view."

Her assignment was simple, direct—get up close and personal with Baxter Remington. Find out what Baxter knew about his now-missing VP's insider trading activities, and the missing man's current location.

Considering Baxter's affinity for blondes with curves, she was the perfect agent for the job. Considering he was James Bond debonair, the assignment wasn't totally unappealing. Not that she was anything but professional. That said, Baxter's appeal did nothing to change how much she despised being used for her looks. She always paid the price later—less respect from a partner who had barely offered her any to start with. That really ticked her off.

She was good at her job, top of her class at the academy, promoted long before many of her peers. And she wanted another promotion, far away from this place and her partner's abuse. Baxter Remington was her ticket to that promotion. Snag him and his VP, and she'd snag opportunity and an exit from hell.

Time for action—she stepped around a Christmas tree decorated with brilliant, albeit costume, diamonds and pearls, and intercepted a waiter. Perfectly timed, Sarah managed to reach for the champagne tray at the same moment Baxter did. Their hands collided and she laughed, low, sexy.

"Sorry about that," she said, casting him an interested look.

He gave her a half smile. It lacked the returned interest she'd hoped for. "Ladies first," he offered, motioning to the tray.

She accepted a glass from the waiter and watched as Baxter did the same. Expectantly, she waited for the server to leave, waited for Baxter's affinity for flirtation to kick in. Instead, she found him turning away, watching the stage.

Fred, her partner and the agent in her earpiece, spoke. "Sarah, honey, you are going to have to do better than that." Fred hated female agents. Or maybe he just hated her. She wanted to tell him what she thought of him, but professionally, this was not the time, or the place.

Sarah blew a long lock of silvery blond hair out of her eyes. She'd sprayed it with just enough silver sparkle to bring attention to her dress and her ample cleavage. She'd really put herself out to look like

Baxter's ideal fantasy. Baxter had a thing for blondes; it was well-known. As a favorite of the local press, he was often photographed with a blonde flavor-of-the-month dangling from his arm.

The announcer came to the stage. The runway show was starting. A reporter appeared in front of Baxter, drilling him over the accusations of his VP's insider trading activities. Sneaky bastard had managed to snag an invitation to the party. *He should be working for the Feds,* she thought. Sarah flagged another waiter and told him to call security, quickly easing her way to Baxter's side and bringing his conversation with the reporter within hearing range.

"Mr. Remington," the reporter said. "I find it hard to believe that your VP is your closest friend and yet you knew nothing of his actions."

"Frankly," Baxter stated, "I don't give a rat's ass what you believe."

Sarah smoothly linked her arm to his. "Security is on its way, sugar," she said, glaring at the reporter, who cursed and searched the crowd. Sure enough, a pair of security guards were rushing in their direction. The reporter darted away.

She glanced up at Baxter, saw the heaviness of his stare, the disinterest. Damn. What did it take to get this man hot?

"I'm Sarah," she said, leaning into him so that her breast brushed his arm. She used her real name as often as possible. It was easier to avoid screwups that way. "I gather you're Baxter Remington."

He stared down at her, no sign of emotion, an inde-cipherable mask on his handsome face. He disengaged his arm from hers. "Thanks for the save, Sarah. Now, if you'll excuse me. I don't want to miss the show."

The first model was taking the stage, and just like that, he walked away. She watched him weave through the crowd, edging closer to the stage.

Sarah's efforts at seduction had been fruitless.

"I guess he doesn't prefer all blondes, babe," Fred said into the mike.

"Jerk," she hissed, working her way through the crowd toward an empty spot at the food table, where she could speak more freely.

"Save the sweet talk for later, honey," Fred said. "Right now, we need someone close to Baxter Remington. Since you can't do it, we'd better hope one of the other ladies in that joint can. And when she does, we'll snag her, and convince her to help us."

"I'm not your honey or your sweetie," she replied. Unfortunately, she wasn't Baxter's, either.

"Yeah, well—"

She set her plate down and reached up and flipped off her mike, tired of Fred's mouth. Turning to the room, Sarah took in the glitter and glam, and hoped like hell some lucky girl would score with Baxter, as Sarah had not. Because that lady's score would be Sarah's score, as well. They'd both get their man.

And then Sarah could get rid of Fred.

AFTER THAT DISTASTEFUL encounter with the reporter, all that kept Baxter from leaving the charity event was the prospect of another glimpse of the mystery woman wearing the pink sweats. As for the blonde's blatant flirtation, she might not be a reporter, though he wouldn't rule it out. An opportunist of some type, regardless. Been there, done that, not interested.

Impatient, staring at the stage, Baxter's mind flickered to the questions the reporter had flung in his direction. He was sick and tired of the accusations directed at his personal character, tainting the reputation of a company he had worked into a solid success. A company that he'd committed to the mission of giving back to the community at every opportunity. Yet, now, thanks to a trusted employee, he was seeing that reputation, that foundation he'd fought so hard for, smashed into oblivion.

"And as Audrey Hepburn, we have the lovely owner of the Book Nook, Caron Avery."

With that announcement, Baxter's eyes riveted to the stage; all thoughts of the reporter, of the scandal haunting him, slid away. Caron Avery was the mystery woman, and she owned a bookstore. He found that charming for reasons he didn't understand, any more than he understood the overwhelmingly complete way the woman had taken him by storm. When was the last time his gut had twisted with anticipation over seeing a woman? The fact that Caron Avery had excited such a response had become the reason he was still here.

His heart raced as the brunette at the end of the runway appeared; his limbs heated. What would she look like transformed into a starlet? But then he was quite partial to that little pink sweat suit for reasons he couldn't begin to understand. A smile lifted the corners of his mouth as he thought of the way it hugged her cute, firm backside with delicious precision. Okay, maybe he did know what he liked about it.

A female appeared at the edge of the runway and began to sashay toward the crowd. Baxter inhaled, savoring the moment, anticipating the thrum of fire in his veins. The fire that never came. He frowned. This wasn't the woman he'd met at the valet podium. He knew it with the same certainty that he knew those pink sweats had made him hot. The woman on the runway was taller than his mystery woman; she walked with heavier steps, her hips and breasts, fuller.

Baxter cursed under his breath, disappointment curling in his gut. Disappointment that was no more explainable, no more logical, than the over-the-top interest that a chance meeting with a stranger had created in him.

"Correction, ladies and gentlemen," the announcer said. "Caron Avery will be with us later in the show. We've had some last-minute costume changes due to a missing model. In the role of Audrey Hepburn is Suzie Cantu, one of the staffers from the event. What a trouper she is. Whisked onto the runway with no warning!"

The tension in Baxter's shoulders slid away. A waiter appeared and offered him a glass of champagne, and he decided to indulge—that glass of bubbly wasn't the only thing he planned to indulge in. There was a woman on his mind, a woman who had his attention, a woman he had to have. Instinctively, he knew she wasn't a woman for casual bedroom encounters—the only thing his life allowed at the moment. She might want him, but he was certain she would hesitate to act. He would simply have to convince her of the value, the pleasure, of a night of sensual escape. She would be a challenge, a provocative chase he couldn't wait to get underway.

"TIME TO HEAD TO THE STAGE, honey." The brassy yell came from behind her as Betsy appeared in the mirror behind Caron and whistled. "I do declare, missy. You make a damn good Marilyn Monroe."

Did she? Caron wasn't sure. The transformation had happened so quickly, her mind was spinning. She stared at herself in the mirror, amazed at what she saw, amazed at herself. The woman in the reflection wasn't her—but yet, it was. She would never have thought that blond hair would suit her coloring, but with the right makeup and the ruby-red lipstick, she had to admit it appeared she could pull it off.

Then there was her clingy sparkling gown that some-how seemed to create curves that weren't there before, hugging her waist, and caressing her hips. As for her breasts—well, gel bras were, indeed, the true miracle bras. And the low cut of the gown showed plenty of cleavage. Too much. Oh, yeah, too much. How could she walk out on the stage with so much chest showing?

She whirled around and motioned to her chest. "I can't go out there like this."

"Looking sexy?" Betsy asked. "Of course you can!"

Her hands covered her breasts. "They are so exposed."

Betsy laughed. "They are not," she scoffed, one hand on a cocked hip. "You look *elegant* sexy, not slutty sexy. You, darlin', are the show in this showcase. You look amazing."

This was not going as planned. "I was supposed to wear the other dress. The one with the high neckline."

"You wilted in that dress," Betsy said. "You shine in this one."

Oh, God. Her neckline concerns slid away as a new worry took their place. "What if I fall?"

"You won't fall!"

Her stomach rolled. "I fell during high school graduation. People laughed. They laughed a long time. And loud."

Betsy paled, clearly rattled, but it didn't keep her from pushing onward. "Think of this as a challenge. Take over the room like you do your business. Just go out there and forget the crowd, and be Marilyn!"

Betsy really did not understand. "Unless there is a list I can check off and a plan I can follow, I don't do challenge. I do planning, organization. Structure. High necklines." Caron shook her head. "No. No, I don't do last-minute, daring things. It's not me." She waved her hand over the dress again, pointing at her exposed chest. "I. Don't. Do. This." She was starting to hyperventilate. She hadn't done that since college. Not since she'd tried hypnosis. "I can't. I—"

"You can," Betsy argued.

"Can't…breathe," Caron wheezed. "I can't…breathe."

"Step aside! Step aside! She's hyperventilating." Reginald rushed forward with a bag. He started to hold it to her mouth and hesitated. "Watch the lipstick." She grabbed the bag, and he said, "That's it, breathe."

"We have three minutes," Betsy announced, and now she sounded as if *she* might hyperventilate. "If we don't get her out there, *I* am going to need that bag."

Reginald held up a hand. "Wait," he murmured, and focused on Caron. He dropped the bag, put his hands on Caron's shoulders. "My therapist, also known as my older sister, taught me a trick. Imagine—"

She could breathe just enough to cut him off. "Don't say 'the audience in their underwear' or I'll scream."

He pursed his lips and ignored the interruption, as if it did not justify a response. "Shut your eyes." She hesitated and he grimaced and put some authority into his voice. "Snap. Them. Shut. We're out of time."

She grimaced right back, but did as he said. It was better than going out on that stage.

"Now," he said. "I want you to imagine yourself inside a red glowing circle. A protective circle."

Her eyes went wide. This wasn't unfamiliar. "You've done hypnosis."

He pursed his lips. "Snap those eyes shut and imagine the circle."

She inhaled a heavy breath and did as he said.

"Inside your circle is your safe zone. No one can hurt you, no one can laugh, and you cannot and will not fall down. You can be anything you want, *do* anything you want. You can be Marilyn. You can be daring, be challenged. You can live the fantasy."

She repeated his words in her mind, not about the damn red circle, but about how silly she must seem right now. As if a red circle would help her? Please. Hypnosis hadn't done nearly as much for her as the idea of needing it had.

Shoot. Why did she freak out like this? Why couldn't she be Marilyn for a night? Why couldn't she live the fantasy? She opened her eyes. She *could* live the fantasy! She would live the fantasy. She was going to walk that runway, and meet any challenge that came her way that night with bold daring.

Baxter Remington and everyone else in that room—beware! Marilyn Monroe aka Caron Avery was headed their way.

# 3

HOURS AFTER CARON had walked out on that stage, she prudently nursed her second glass of champagne, the sparkling liquid tickling her tongue, the party around her abuzz with food, friends and chatter. Caron herself was abuzz with a titillating game of cat and mouse, which had ensued shortly after her surprisingly successful walk down that stage. A game of Hunter and Huntress, with she and Baxter Remington exchanging heated stares, connecting with an electricity that defied reason. There was no conversation, no attempts at contact, the anticipation heightening with each glance. It excited, it entranced. It promised pleasure long overdue.

She wanted him. The steamy looks he'd cast her way, the heavy-lidded stares, said he wanted her, too. No doubt, he had no idea she was the woman in those pink sweats. She barely knew that woman herself right now. Didn't want to know her. That woman would be logical and prim; that woman would not blatantly flirt with Baxter Remington, even from a distance, as she had done often this evening.

"The economy is not improving. I think…"

Caron blinked, realizing she was involved in a conversation she had forgotten. A short, balding man named Lou, a commercial real estate agent of some sort, was rambling on about office space rates.

She nodded, made a lame comment, her gaze flickering again to the man standing at the bar in the corner, to the Hunter. God, the man was hot. Tall. Dark. Suave in all ways, masculine and sexy.

Her eyes locked with his, her body heating, skin tingling. She could feel her nipples pebble beneath the sheer fabric. Another time, another day, she would have covered herself and been shy rather than boldly female. But she had become the game, become Marilyn. And she was loving every second, embracing the freedom, the power of being "woman."

The flirtation had become an alluring distraction as had the game of control. She was having fun with the sexy bombshell image that she would leave at the door at the end of the enchanting evening. For now, she reveled in the freedom that came with the role she was playing. Once she'd pressed past her nerves, once she'd embraced Marilyn, she'd found the experience quite absorbing, found it alluringly sexy. But the most alluring part of all was knowing *he* was watching. Knowing she had the ability to make him watch.

A tiny ache budded between her thighs with a discomfort that demanded attention. Caron sipped her champagne, the bubbles floating down her throat. She had a buzz that delivered courage. A buzz that sizzled with a cry for satisfaction. That called out for action. It was time to escalate this flirtation, to find out exactly how far it would travel.

She shifted her attention to the conversation, nodded

and exchanged a few words before excusing herself. She didn't look toward her Hunter. Didn't have to. She could feel him staring at her, feel him as surely as she could the tingling of her skin, the sizzle of her sensitized nerve endings. How long had it been since she had felt the touch of a man's hand, felt the pleasure of intimately joined bodies? She needed that feeling, needed it as surely as she needed her next breath.

Caron weaved through the thinning crowd; the hour was growing late, near midnight. Her destination was the courtyard at the rear of the elegant entertainment room, as she murmured a few greetings along the way.

She pushed open the double-paned doors and exited, the cool air sweeping her hot skin, enveloping her with temporary relief. Fancy stone benches and fragrant sweet flowers lined the red brick trail, ground lights illuminating the colors of red, yellow and white. Caron didn't linger, pressing forward, down the path, into the shadows. The click of the door sounded behind her, and a shiver tingled its way down her spine. *He* was there. He followed.

BAXTER STEPPED INTO the night air, the wind lifting around him, his eyes catching on the silky swirl of material a second before it disappeared down the fork to the left, hidden by decorative foliage. He smiled, the Hunter in him on the prowl. For her, his little contradiction. The woman beneath the seductive Marilyn Monroe persona, who was also his little brunette butterfly. Innocence and seduction. The contrast intrigued him. But what really intrigued him was what he felt deep in his gut when he peered across the room at her, the deep swirl of desire that tightened his groin and maddened him with need.

He inhaled, took in the night air, tasted it—savoring the flavor of passion and perfume thick on his tongue— her perfume, her passion. He stepped forward, tension in his muscles, desire in his blood. Long strides took him down the path—slow, steady strides that defied the urgency pulsing within his groin. Control was a talent, a game-winning tool in all aspects of life, certainly in the art of pleasure. The more anticipation, the more wanting, the more relish in the ultimate moment of release.

He turned the corner, cut back through the darkness illuminated with little lights dangling above the brick path, teetering on black steel poles. His nostrils flared as the sweet smell of floral-scented passion thickened. One more step, two. Three. And then he paused at the end of the path, the vision before him breathtaking. A glorious view of the San Francisco Bridge opened up to him, the moon shining in the deep black sky, framing a vision of one single, blonde goddess.

She leaned against the railing, the breeze gently blowing, exposing creamy white skin. Would it be as soft as he thought it would be? Would she taste of sugar or spice? Would she purr like a kitten or scream like a cat? A kitten, he thought. He couldn't wait to find out for sure. Still, he didn't rush, didn't push forward. Baxter lingered to enjoy the vision of pure female love-liness before him. Enjoyed considering all the erotic possibilities the two of them could share. Enjoyed trailing his eyes along the zipper of her dress, imagining drawing it downward, moments before he tugged away the silky material. Moments before he exposed bare skin and full, high breasts. His eyes traveled the long line of her silhouette one last time, the tapered, tiny waist, the curves of her lush hips. She didn't turn, didn't move, yet somehow he felt her awareness of his presence.

His lips lifted slightly, the thrum of excitement roused by the coyness of her keeping her back to him. With slow precision, he closed the distance between himself and the blonde seductress, his pace a part of retaining his mandatory, ironclad control—control that defied the demands of his body. Just as slowly, Caron turned and faced him, presenting him with further reason for urgency. He stopped mere steps from touching her. His gaze rasped along the low-cut dress, caressing her breasts, noting the taut nipples pressed against the thin, white silk.

His eyes lifted to her full, red lips, parted with anticipation, with invitation. The bright color contrasted with her pale skin as perfectly as did her dark, full lashes. He wanted to kiss those lips. He wanted to taste her, to please her. He wanted to tell her everything he longed to do to her, intended to do to her. But something in her eyes kept him from speaking. A flash of fear, a split second where she was a doe in the headlights. Insecure. Nervous. He didn't remember the last time he'd seen such things in a woman. Had he ever? Those things touched him deeply, aroused him profoundly.

Silence became his weapon of seduction. Silence held no demands; it came without questions, without consequence, without reasons to think rather than to feel. He could see those needs in her eyes, see that she was acting out of character, acting out the fantasy of the costume, against the more sensible decisions of her true self. And the fact that she'd chosen to step outside her own personal boundaries and do so with him only served to ignite a primal possessiveness in him. A desire to make her his—if only for one night. A desire that urged him to reach for her, but he did not, yet.

Instinct told him he had a choice to make. He could wait and allow her to act—but did he dare risk her running, risk her darting away? Perhaps he should press forward, take what he wanted—take her pleasure and take her passion—take her on a ride to satisfaction she would never forget. He considered a moment, the deep thrum of desire pulsing through his veins, primal fire pumping with each beat of his heart.

The hunt was over but the game had only just begun.

CARON HAD SET THE STAGE for the courtyard seduction, yet she could barely breathe as Baxter Remington leaned on the railing next to her, smelling like cinnamon and spice, and oh, yes, everything nice. The man simply oozed sex appeal, the confident playboy and millionaire. "Caron logic" said she was way over her head, a lamb playing a wolf's game. The buzz of champagne, gel bra and a successful walk down that runway, said she was empowered, living a fantasy where she owned the game.

"It's a city made for lovers," he said softly, the heaviness of his attentive stare caressing her bare skin as she slid into position beside him, her hands dangling over the railing.

"And a night made for fantasies," she replied, staring out at the magnificence of the San Francisco Bridge, its structure seeming to float atop the endless mass of dark water. She tilted her chin to her left, met Baxter's expression, the depths of passion she found there stripping away any and all barriers in a tantalizingly sensual way.

"Is that what this is?" he asked, facing her, casually leaning on the rail, though there was nothing casual about the tension crackling in the air, nor the lavish promise of pleasure that lifted in the midst of that crackle. "A fantasy?"

Caron eased around to face him, the moon and the stars shadowing the chiseled angles of his face, adding mystery to his suave allure. Her mouth watered as she took in his hotness factor. He was one of those rare men who made a tux sexy, rather than the opposite.

"You have a problem with fantasies?" she challenged softly, her voice somewhere between confident and uncertain.

His lips lifted in a barely perceivable, ultrasexy way. "No problem with fantasies whatsoever."

"Good," she said and ran her teeth over her bottom lip, nerve endings she didn't know existed, raw and tingling. "Because I'm—"

A gust of wind blew through the thin material of her dress, and Caron lost her thought, curling into herself, and shivering in the process.

As would be expected of a gallant knight in a fantasy—and Baxter was most certainly that—he quickly shrugged out of his jacket and wrapped it around her shoulders, using the lapels to pull her close. His body sheltered her, warmed her in intimate places.

"A city made for lovers," he said, repeating his earlier words. "Sometimes I think it's alive. That it lives and breathes romance and seduction. That well-timed breeze did, after all, give me the perfect excuse to pull you closer."

A new shiver chased a path down her spine, and this one had nothing to do with the cool night. "I wouldn't think a man like Baxter Remington needs an excuse to take what he wants."

He arched a brow. "And why is that?"

"Rich, successful owner of a major coffee company," she replied without hesitation—after all, she was stating pure fact. "You didn't get there by waiting for an excuse to act."

Sultry, attentive eyes met hers. Oh, yes. She wanted to lick this man from head to toe. She swallowed hard, realizing how out of character her thinking was. Actually, she should expect Baxter to do the licking, not the opposite. Maybe there would be time for both? She bit her lip. Perhaps she should settle for another glass of champagne. Yes. That was probably the more appropriate response. Than licking him. All over. Right. Champagne.

She blinked up at him, realizing Baxter had said something, and tried to disguise the blatant desire, no doubt ablaze in her eyes. "I'm sorry. What?"

Amusement lit his handsome features, as if he knew she'd been in naughty fantasyland instead of listening. He gently tugged the lapels of his coat with enough force to insist she step closer. So close they were almost touching. Their legs, their hips. Her chin tilted upward, seeking confirmation that he felt the charge tingling along her nerve endings. Her attention focused on his mouth. Firm. Sexy. She wanted to kiss him.

"It hardly seems fair that you know so much more about me than I know about you," he commented softly.

It was an obvious nudge to reveal the woman beneath the costume, but Caron wasn't a fool. She recognized that too much Caron in this equation meant bye-bye fantasy and a chance to enjoy this hunk of a man. Caron wasn't letting that happen. She smiled coyly.

"I like it that way," she replied, flattening her hand on the warm, solid wall of his chest to keep from melting against him. Muscles flexed beneath her fingers. Somehow she managed to find her voice again. "Yes," she murmured, repeating her words. "I like it that way. Me knowing more about you than you about me."

His hand covered hers, holding her palm over his heart. "Is that so?"

She nodded slowly. "It is," she assured him. "After all, tonight I'm Cinderella, or rather Marilyn. It's my fantasy, which means I set the rules."

"And who says it's your fantasy?" he asked, a hint of amusement in his tone. "Why can't it be mine?"

"I'm the one in costume," she quickly reminded him. "If you go put on a nice pirate costume, I'll let it be your fantasy."

A sexy rumble of deep laughter followed. "I'll keep that in mind for future reference," he said. "But for the record, I have a variety of fantasies forming that I might well feel compelled to make come true—none of which involve a pirate's costume." His lips lifted. "Though I'm not ruling out anything." His eyes danced with mischief. "But in light of these fantasies, I'll have to request you be up-front about my boundaries—'the rules,' as you called them," his seductive voice whispered. "That way I don't forget myself and say…kiss you, when you might prefer I simply do this." He slid his hands to her waist and began nuzzling her neck. "Hmm," he murmured next to her ear. "You smell like roses." His hands caressed a path up her back.

Caron embraced the solid wall of muscle in a tidal wave of sensation.

"Kissing me would definitely be out of line." She pressed her hands to his powerful shoulders, and slid them slowly downward, absorbing every flex and line with slow intent. "I can't have my lipstick messed up when I have to go back inside."

He smiled against her neck. "We couldn't have that, now could we?"

"Excuse me, Miss, well, Ms. Monroe," came a gentle female voice that jerked Caron backward as her gaze skittered and landed on a petite brunette she recognized as one of the event organizers.

"Hi," Caron replied, more than a little flustered. She started to push away from Baxter but quickly caught herself. What had happened to her confidence, her allure? She'd just been caught with the sexiest man in the building. Instead of fleeing, she rotated in Baxter's arms, held the jacket in place, while he wrapped a possessive arm around her waist beneath it. "Did you need me?"

Appearing nervous, the woman's gaze skittered from Baxter to Caron. "I do apologize for the interruption and for not having your given name handy," the woman said, wringing her fingers together. "But the last dance of the night is about to start and it's televised. There's quite the panic to find you."

Caron offered a reassuring smile. "I'll be there in a minute."

The woman nodded and rushed away in a frenzied half run. Baxter returned to nuzzling Caron's neck, the touch of his lips on the sensitive flesh. She pressed her hands on his chest, to put at least some distance between them. She wasn't about to be an easy catch, no matter how much she longed for this man. This wasn't about falling at this guy's feet. She could do that any day. This was about the high of having him fall at hers. About enjoying the power of her newfound sexuality before this night ended.

She peered up at him through her lashes, those sultry bedroom eyes inviting her back into a world of silk sheets and naked bodies—their naked bodies. "The final dance of the night is always the best, you know," she said, hardly believing what she was about to say. Did she dare?

One dark brow arched. "And why exactly is that?"

Caron's throat thickened at the cue for her reply and silently inhaled, channeling her new persona and forcefully shoving aside her nerves. Be daring, Caron, she told herself. She ran her hands down his tie—she liked that he'd chosen a conventional tie over a bow tie. Liked the sprinkle of gray at his sideburns. She liked a lot about this man, she thought.

Finally she said, "Everyone knows the guy who gets the last dance takes the girl home." Her voice was soft, sexy. The challenge in the words unfamiliar, yet surprisingly comfortable. She rather enjoyed the freedom to say what she was thinking.

Baxter rewarded her lack of reserve by tugging her closer, thighs aligned with hers, warmth radiating through her limbs despite a sudden gust of evening wind.

"Sweetheart," he said. "As honored as I would be to be your last dance, the last thing you want is to be photographed as my latest conquest and splashed all over the papers."

Caron's eyes went wide at the unexpected, and not-so-satisfying bite of those words. She was no born Marilyn, but she was woman enough to know Baxter Remington had just earned himself a justified smackdown in the name of every woman in this place. And she intended to give it to him.

A slow, confident smile slid onto red-painted lips. "Ah now, darling," she purred. "The only one in danger of being a conquest this night is you." She pushed to her toes and brought her lips a breath from his, teasing him with the potential kiss. "And that is still up for debate."

She pulled back, denying him her mouth, pleased at the stunned look gracing his chiseled features. She slid off his coat and pressed it into his hands, leaning into him as she did and allowing a nice view of her gel-induced, ogleworthy cleavage, while she still had it.

"Thanks for the jacket," she told him, her lips pursing ever so slightly. "And the company." Desire flared in his eyes, and he reached for her. She took a fast step backward, then two.

"Final dance to attend," she reminded him, wiggling her fingers in a sultry wave, and then she turned and started walking—no, strutting—just as she had on the runway. A sexy, empowered sort of walk she'd never even attempted before tonight but found to be liberating.

Caron could feel the heat of Baxter's stare, the way he watched every sway of her hips, every slow, calculated step. Oh, yeah. She'd taught him a lesson. He was going to have to work to be her arm candy. And she had no doubt, he would. She'd seen the shocked look on his face, the flare of renewed desire that had followed—she would be seeing more of Baxter Remington before this night of Marilyn ended.

## 4

CALLING CARON A CONQUEST had been a slip of the tongue brought on by the bitter taste of media hell, a hell that he couldn't drag her into for just a night of fantasy. A slip that she was making him pay for, and pay well.

Thirty minutes after being left alone in that courtyard, wishing he could pull back his slight, Baxter was propped against a bar near the dance floor, nursing a barely touched scotch, and pretending nonchalance he didn't feel. He sipped the amber-colored liquor and watched as Rich Reynolds, the CEO of a major telecomm—a man known for running through women as fast as he did board members—danced with Caron in far too intimate an embrace, the damn Dean Martin holiday tune apparently never coming to an end.

That he fought a possessive desire to interrupt Caron's dance and claim it as his own despite the media frenzy sure to follow, spoke volumes about how completely this woman had taken him by storm. Caron and Marilyn had successfully seduced him—one woman, in two completely different ways. And if that one woman had been anyone but Caron, he'd think she was playing him, and playing him like a pro. But he'd seen Caron in her natural form, experienced the pure honesty that slid from her lush little mouth, regardless of consequence, as she'd rambled adorably on about toilets and *his* high-priced coffee. Leading him to the firm belief that her Marilyn persona had not been the one to put him in his place. The response had been too natural, too quick. It had been the real Caron, the natural woman.

She'd put him in his place, and let him know that as easily as she had invited him into her fantasy, she could set him aside. Well. He had no intention of being set aside. So he was biding his time, waiting until the right moment to approach her again—knowing she expected as much and being remarkably okay with that.

He sipped his drink, watched with agitation as Rich slowly brushed the top of Caron's lush backside. He ground his teeth. "Oh, hell." Before Baxter could stop himself, he charged toward the dance floor and made his way to Caron's side. He tapped Rich's shoulder and leaned forward, "Cutting in."

Caron's eyes went wide, but lit with the hint of appreciation he'd hoped for. Rich, on the other hand, cast him a go-to-hell look. "Sorry, bud," Rich retorted. "Last dance is a complete dance."

"Let's let the lady decide," Baxter argued, standing his ground.

Both men's eyes fell on Caron, and she visibly swallowed hard. Then, motioned toward Baxter. "I did promise you the last dance," she offered and shrugged out of Rich's arms, graciously adding, "Thank you for the dance, Rich."

Rich had the nerve to look as if he might refuse to step aside, which sat none too well with Baxter. He quickly slid his arm around Caron's waist and directed her toward the center of the dance floor, away from the disgruntled CEO.

Caron laughed, her expression lighting with a spontaneous, engaging, smile. "That was rude," she chided. "And I thought you couldn't dance with me because of the media frenzy?"

"I shouldn't be," he agreed, molding her closer. She was a petite package of softness and curves. Even in her stilettos, her head barely reached his shoulders. "But I wasn't about to leave his hand on your lovely backside." His own hand rested dangerously close on her lower back. He wanted her naked, that ass firmly in his palms.

"It seems to me your hand is in the exact same spot," she challenged with a lift of her chin and enough uncertainty in her eyes to tell him she was struggling to act her role. His groin tightened. Why did that vulnerability in her turn him on so?

"But you want my hand there," he countered gently, cautiously taking the bait, no desire to scare her off.

She blushed despite her sexy persona but managed to keep him on his toes with a challenge. "So another man's hand is enough to make you forget your media phobia?"

"Apparently," he told her, the soft scent of woman flaring in his nostrils. "And considering the scandal my company is going through, that's not an easy task."

She fixed him with a suspicious look. "What scandal?"

His eyes held hers, welcoming her to see the honesty there. "Nothing you'd wish to be a part of," he assured her, their hips swaying in a slow rhythm, legs intimately entwined. He wanted them naked and entwined. "Believe me, I wanted nothing more than to share your last dance. I was trying to protect you." He pressed his cheek to hers, lips near her ear. "What man wouldn't want to be Marilyn Monroe's public conquest?"

She shivered in his arms—so damn responsive it drove him wild. Her hand flattened on his chest as she inched backward and challenged, "I thought *I* was the conquest?"

"I was thinking it would be rather fun to compete for that honor," he suggested. "Privately."

She considered that and then motioned toward the table not far away. "See the feisty redhead yelling at the tall, thin man?"

His gaze took in the woman with a tape measure and sewing kit of some sort around her neck. "The one who looks like she's about to blow a gasket?" he asked, curiosity piqued at the odd shift in conversation.

Caron's hands settled on his upper arms, framing her cleavage in a deliciously inviting way as she said, "She's waiting to strip away Marilyn as soon as this dance ends."

Baxter's gaze narrowed on Caron, searching her lovely features for confirmation of what he believed he understood—she didn't want anyone but him to strip away Marilyn. "We can't have that, now can we?"

She drew a discreet breath that he didn't miss, a sign of nerves he vowed to pleasure away. "What do you propose?"

He wiggled a brow. "The great escape, of course," he offered. "You game?"

A slow smile slid onto her face. "Lead the way."

BEFORE CARON UNDERSTOOD WHAT WAS happening, Baxter was weaving through the crowd, sidestepping one attempt at communication after another until he pulled her down a hallway and into a stairwell. The next thing she knew, they were cutting through the kitchen, and approaching one of the busboys. Her eyes went wide as she realized Baxter was speaking to him in Spanish—damn, could the man get any sexier? A second later, he handed the man cash, and then whisked her into the staff elevator and pushed the button for the basement level.

Caron laughed as Baxter leaned against the wall, tugged her against his long, hard body and settled one hand on her lower back as he had done several times before, fingers barely brushing her backside. Again, nerves clamored within her, but Caron was living on the high of the moment, fears forgotten. "I can't believe you got us out of there so fast. What did you say to the busboy?"

"A limo is picking us up in the basement."

Her jaw dropped. "Limo?"

His finger trailed over her lower lip and goose bumps chased a path along her spine. "Nothing less for Marilyn, right? And it will throw at least a few people off our trail."

Before Caron could process this announcement, the elevator opened on the basement parking level. Caron turned in Baxter's arms to find the limo ready and waiting, back door open. Her heart raced, all the nerves she'd combated this night suddenly colliding in an instant of panic. She couldn't do this! What the heck was she thinking?

How could she compare to the women of his past?

Of his future? Her. Little Caron Avery, whose college boyfriend had been more interested in books than sex, and when he'd gotten around to the sex part—well, the books had been better. The few other men—improvements, but still nothing grand.

Walking a runway without falling down did not make her a seductress ready to take on a man like Baxter Remington, no matter how fancy the costume. She started to bolt, to seek escape, but warm, powerful arms wrapped around her from behind. "Does the car meet your satisfaction?"

Caron swallowed hard, Baxter's breath tickling her ear, her neck. "Oh, yes," she whispered, thinking more than the car met her satisfaction. The man did, too. Because no man had ever affected her like Baxter. A look, a touch, a simple word spoken in that deep baritone voice, and she was ready to give herself to him. The reaction he created in her was both terrifying and thrilling in the same breath.

"That's what I was hoping you would say," Baxter replied, and walked her forward, toward the car, that big, delicious body still draped around hers.

She was getting in that limo with him, she realized, and not because he wanted her to. Because she wanted to, because she'd come so far tonight—too far to toss away the ultimate reward—and that reward was not Baxter. He was simply the man who fit the fantasy, and that fantasy was about being daring. Daring to let go of her inhibitions, if only for one night. And even better, a night that came with benefits to her business. This night wasn't self-indulgent. It was about a better future, a better bookstore, a more confident self.

Caron was taking the fantasy to a whole new level.

THE MINUTE THE LIMO pulled away, Sarah exited from the shadows and crossed to a van parked in the dark corner spot, lights out. The back doors popped open—Fred had obviously noted her approach—and she lifted her skirt to awkwardly climb inside, not missing the raised eyebrow Fred cast her way as she flashed him, her legs embarrassingly wide at the time. Of course, he wasn't about to let it go, either, non-gentleman that he was.

"Easy now, darlin'," he taunted. "I'm not the target."

"Just tell me you've got the background on Marilyn," Sarah grumbled, turning away to shut the door so he wouldn't see the flush of her cheeks. She had no idea why she let the man get to her, but he did. And in his normal irritating refusal to be dismissed, he appeared by her side and pulled the other door shut, their hands colliding in an awkward charge of electricity.

For just an instant, she blinked at those big brown eyes framed by a few strands of light brown hair slipped free from the tie at the back of his neck, and like always, she felt that familiar punch in her gut. The one that made her want to punch him in the gut for making her feel such a thing. He was everything she hated in the agency, a man who made being a female agent feel as if her presence was breaking the rules, as if she didn't belong.

"I could have gotten inside fine by myself," she said foully, distancing herself with as much grace as she could, yet managing to stick her ass right in his incredibly not handsome, though somehow ruggedly alluring, face. She looked over her shoulder as he lifted his big hand to have a smack.

"Don't you dare," she said, jerking around to sit in the chair in front of a monitor—exactly where he should be focused, instead of on giving her hell.

A low, baritone chuckle escaped his lips. "You really are in a foul mood," he said, claiming the chair next to her, the rip in his faded denim jeans displaying a light sprinkle of brown hair probably the same color as the hair on his chest.

Why was she thinking about his chest hair? "Damn it," Sarah murmured, jerking her gaze to the closed notebook computer in front of her and opening it.

Fred frowned. "Your computer crash again?"

"No," she ground out between her teeth. "We do have a man on that limo, right?"

He pointed to a monitor on the far left. "The limo service will be calling us with the drop-off location."

Good, she thought. "What about Marilyn? You have anything on her yet?"

"I had it the minute Baxter made it clear he had eyes for no one but her, hours ago," he said, as he punched a few keys and sent data to her computer. "And she's as squeaky clean as they come." He punched another few keys. "Caron Avery owns a bookstore on the corner of Anchor and 2nd Street. Workaholic. Barely dates. Before her store, she worked for Barnes & Noble. She visits her grandmother in Sonoma every other week. Has no living parents. No siblings. Doesn't own a pet, though has been known to volunteer at the local animal shelter. Doesn't even have a parking ticket. Not one. Ever. In her life."

"Look harder. There has to be something we can use to motivate her to help." Sarah tabbed through the file. "What about a friend in trouble we can help as a reward for her assistance?"

He shook his head. "A small list, carefully selected," he replied. "They're all as shiny and nice as she is." He ran big hands down his thighs and leaned back in the metal chair. "It's all there. Check me if you like."

"I will," she said, scanning the screen.

"There's no guarantee this will go beyond tonight," he said. "I say wait until tomorrow and see what happens."

"Unless something goes drastically wrong tonight, he'll be back."

"You can't know that."

"I saw up close and personal how he looked at her."

"You mean how he didn't look at you."

Sarah ignored his remark. "What about employees? Anything we can use there?"

"She has one and she's college age and never been in a lick of trouble. We have zilch to motivate her to help." Lick. He used that word just to get at her. She hated it. She'd told him so. Sarah ignored it this time, too rattled by her personal failure with Baxter to keep up with Fred. "Just her duty to help us as an upstanding, good citizen which it sounds like she takes seriously."

Fred snorted. "You're wasting your time with this chick. Strip away the costume and she loses the security blanket. She'll wilt into a wallflower."

Instantly, Sarah stiffened. How many women had been made to feel like either a wallflower or trophy, compliments of some man. She frowned.

"A costume does not make a woman," she argued. "Confidence does." *And experience,* Sarah thought, but Caron would have that after tonight. "Caron Avery can handle Baxter Remington if she puts her mind to it." She hoped.

# 5

CARON SETTLED ON THE LIMO SEAT, when much to her dismay, the front slit split wide, exposing leg all the way to the top of the lacy thigh-highs. She sucked in a breath and fumbled for her skirt, struggling. Baxter bent down and pulled the silk material together, his touch gentle yet insistent.

He smiled, gentle, playful. "Having trouble?"

She blushed. "Nothing you don't seem to have under control."

His eyes lit. "I aim to please."

Oh, wow, what did she say to that? The man was making her wet just talking. How was she supposed to think? Talking. Right. That worked.

"Talk is cheap, *Mr. Remington,*" she taunted in a remarkably hot voice. She didn't know she could sound like that. She liked it.

He chuckled and gave the driver directions, before scooting her farther inside the car with him following, one long, muscular leg plastered to hers.

A moment later, his hand framed her face, his lips lingering above hers. Good. No talking. She didn't do so well in that category. Right to the kisses. To the pleasure. But he didn't kiss her. His breath tickled her lips, teasing her with the kiss she'd longed for since the moment she'd set eyes on him. He waited, lingered. Teased her. Somehow one of her legs rested across his, their bodies melded intimately. Caron was breathing hard, her chest rising and falling against his, her breasts aching for his touch. Her core tightened with need, her panties wet with the desire that had been building the past few hours for this man—now unleashed.

Never before had Caron forgotten her environment, her control. Never had she wanted a kiss to the point of taking it, and she told herself to wait, to make him come to her. To make him beg.

Suddenly, she didn't care. Caron laced her fingers into his dark, tousled hair and brought his lips to hers. He rewarded her with a long slide of delicious tongue that had her begging for more. Hungrily, she kissed him, hungrily she took his tongue, his mouth. Clung to him when he tore his mouth from hers, blinking in disorientation.

He slid her to a sitting position in the seat, him on one knee in front of her, another seat behind him. He shoved open the front slit of her skirt, exposing her legs again all the way to the lace of her thigh-highs.

Their eyes held and locked, and Caron could barely breathe for the potency of that connection. "Do you know why I stopped kissing you?"

No, but she wanted to. "Why?" she asked, staring into his light brown eyes, unable to look away. It was like indulging in a creamy mixture of melted chocolate, silky smooth and full of pleasure.

"Because," he said, the one word lingering in the air as she reached for the words to follow. "You never told me the rules. I wouldn't want to overstep my boundaries."

She sat back slightly. Oh, yeah. Damn. That had sounded good at the time. But she kind of liked the "no thinking" part of a few moments before. Yep. Really wanted to go back to the lost in abandonment, no thinking, no nerves kind of kissing. "I'll, um, let you know if you're out of line. So far you're doing very well."

He shook his head, those dark, dreamy eyes taking on a dangerously seductive quality. "A smart man learns his boundaries up front." He looked up at her with devilish innocence, his dark hair mussed and begging for her fingers as he said, "So—tell me, *Marilyn*. Can I touch you?"

Could he hear her heart racing, because she was pretty darn certain it was loud enough to reach the driver's distant ears. Where? Where did he want to touch her? She wanted to ask but she wasn't sure how she'd handle his answer. She settled for, "Yes." The one-word reply barely qualified as a whisper.

"Here?" he asked. His palms settled gently on her knees and shot little darts of fire up her thighs.

She squeezed them together, embarrassed by how easily she was aroused. "Yes."

His hand trailed over her calves, leaving goose bumps in their wake before soothing them away as he caressed back up to her knees. Then his palms moved up her thighs until his fingers traced the lace of her thigh-highs, his gaze on the tight V of her body. He skimmed back to her knees and fixed her in a heavy-lidded stare.

"Open for me," he ordered.

She squeezed the tiny gap that his prodding had inadvertently created. She instantly felt the pleasure and fear of his gentle demand. She was excited. She was terrified. She didn't know how to respond. She didn't have to. He was kissing her knees, running his hands down her calves and making her forget words. She shivered with the touch, hungered for more.

"Open baby. I've been thinking about how sweet you'd taste all night."

She barely contained a gasp at the words. No one had ever said something so bold to her before. It scared her how much it turned her on, how out of control she felt. How under his control. Her hands settled on top of his where they rested on her knees, stilling his actions before she forgot to stop him.

He seemed to sense her panic, leaning back on his ankles, his hands sliding away, leaving her wishing for them back. "It's your fantasy, your rules. Tell me what you want."

She bit her bottom lip. She wanted his hands back. She wanted... She knew what she wanted and, damn it, she would not be afraid to ask for it. She lifted her hips before she lost her courage, and slid her panties off, then reached for his hand and pressed them into his palm. "You forgot to take these off first," she stated, amazed and pleased at the confident, sexy voice she issued the reprimand in.

Hunger—deep, dark and profoundly male—slid across his face, and she reveled at her achievement of having put it there. She shifted her skirt aside and opened her knees. "Now, where were we?"

With a look of pure, primal lust etching his chiseled face, he eased out of his jacket and tossed it aside. A slow, sensual smile slid onto his firm lips. "The part where I become your conquest, I believe."

He wasted no time getting to work on her pleasure. His palms pressed a path up her legs, his thumbs teasing her sensitive inner thighs.

His body followed the path his hands were taking, his hips spreading her wider. She welcomed him closer, welcomed his warmth, her arms wrapping around his neck. His mouth found hers at the same instant his thumbs brushed her swollen nub. Caron gasped with shock, and he swallowed it with a slow drag of his mouth across hers. Then another.

His thumbs were replaced by long fingers sliding along the sleek, sensitive flesh of her core, and her hips jerked as one dipped inside her. "So wet, so hot," he murmured against her mouth. His fingers parted her farther, entered her deeper.

"Do these lips taste as good as these?" he said, his teeth nipping at her mouth, his fingers doing something absolutely too good to be described before he added, "Why don't I find out? Yes?"

At her boldest she would not have thought she would answer that question, yet she heard herself say, "Yes."

He leaned back, stared down at her, that pure male hunger she'd seen when she handed him her panties back again. Apparently, he liked it when she asked for things. She'd have to remember that for later.

With satisfaction, she watched as he settled between her legs, the warm heat of his mouth closing down over her clit. Caron felt as if every nerve ending in her body exploded with that contact. Her back arched, her hips lifted, chest thrust in the air. And when her legs were suddenly over his shoulders—little pants of pleasure coming uncontrollably from her lips—she decided this asking-for-what-she-wanted thing was working out pretty nicely for her, as well.

He lapped at her, licking, suckling, teasing. Far more easily than she would have ever imagined, Caron found herself shivering into mindless bliss. She didn't want him to stop. She grabbed for the back of the seat, stared down at his head between her legs. Moaned at the erotic sight it made. He suckled her clit into his mouth and slid a finger inside her, then another. She felt them search her inner wall, caressing, then pumping. Her eyes were heavy, her limbs weightless. Pumping against his hand, his mouth. She didn't want him to stop.

Her hand went to his head but she bit her lip, forced herself not to cling. But that tongue. It was magic. It was… Her fingers laced into his hair. She couldn't help herself. And hung on tight. She was afraid he would stop before she was ready. He couldn't stop. Not yet. Something about the way he lavished her with long, silky strokes was just too good to end. She could feel that little bite of ache that had to be answered, and she pumped against his tongue, against his hand, panting with need. Soon, she shattered; the hard spasms rocked her with so much pleasure that her entire body shook.

With slow perfection, Baxter eased her body into re-laxation, soothing her with slower strokes of his tongue, caressed her down to complete, utter satisfaction, and then, and only then, did he slide his fingers from inside her. He brought her knees together and then settled his hands on top of them, and Caron found herself embarrassed by the intensity of her response to this man.

"Even sweeter than I imagined," he said softly. His words only intensified the heat rushing to her cheeks. Her lashes fluttered, lifted, and she fumbled for the right reply. Should she say thank you? She didn't know. She'd never been given a mind-blowing orgasm like this one, let alone in a public place. "It was, um, nice."

"Nice?" he asked, his features darkening instantly. "Did you just say it was 'nice'?" He wasn't pleased.

Okay. Try again. "Thank you?"

He lifted a brow. "Thank you?"

His eyes darkened, narrowed, and then he moved, his hands pressing into the leather on either side of her knees.

"*Nice* is how you describe the guy you're fixing a friend up with. *Nice* is the guy you went out with and never want to see again. Was it nice?"

Okay. Bad choice of words. She shook her head, swallowed hard. Decided to say to heck with the Marilyn-style slyness and just speak her mind. "Mind-blowing," she said. "It was mind-blowing. Couldn't you tell?"

With a half-veiled look he studied her intently, then moved toward her to brush that firm mouth across hers. "Do you know what I want to do right now?"

Strip her naked and make love to her? "Tell me," she whispered.

"Take you inside my apartment and make you come so many mind-blowing ways, you forget the word *nice* ever existed."

She didn't even know they had started driving, let

alone arrived at his apartment. But it didn't matter. His words—their meaning—were very clear.

"Oh." She mouthed the word, realizing she'd just received her second lesson of the night. Lesson number one had been—tell him what she wanted and he would give it to her. Lesson number two—compliment him after a grand orgasm and he would give her more. Check. Not likely to forget that one.

"Just one special request," he said.

Her heart fluttered, excitement spurring it into erratic action. What did he want? The return of pleasure? Here? Now? "Request?"

"Don't ever use the word *nice* again." And then he kissed her.

BAXTER KICKED THE DOOR of his twentieth-floor apartment shut. Lust, raw and heavy, settled in his gut as he watched Caron step to the edge of the shiny stairwell of six steps leading down to the grand-sized, open room of sleek black leather decor. His gaze swept that heart-shaped perky little ass and his groin tightened, expanding uncomfortably against the steel of his zipper. She was his now. They were alone. A back entrance to the building and well-trained staff had allowed a silent entry into the elite Financial District building. The manned security desk offered extra assurance that no one would reach them from there.

He busied himself with the security panel, reining in his passion, aware she was on unfamiliar ground. If he'd read her right—and he was pretty damn certain he had—she'd need a minute to feel in control. But that control would be as much a facade as her costume. This was his domain, his world, and that was why he'd brought her here despite his policy of never bringing women home. Here he could allow her all the freedom she wanted, without the concern that she'd bolt at any minute.

He took a step toward her and she darted forward, out of reach.

"Nice place you have here," she said, cautiously lifting her skirt as she took the stairs.

Baxter's lips twisted with amusement, his cock thickening with the thrill of the chase as he sauntered down the stairs in willing pursuit. "Glad you approve," he said, aware that bringing her here satisfied the deep possessive burn she created in him.

She stopped in the center of his living room beside the marble coffee table, the marble fireplace behind her adorned with family pictures. A corner wine display was to her right. A few sentimental trinkets were displayed in various locations. She took them all in, held her delicate hands by her sides. "Needs books, though."

He smiled, amused, charmed—hungry to get his hands on her. "Says the librarian." He stepped toward her.

She stepped backward, hit the bar, recovered by leaning back and resting her elbows on the granite surface. The action thrust her chest forward, offering him a lush view of her cleavage. His gaze stalled on her full, ripe breasts.

She kept talking. "Books are sexy," she said, her voice hoarser now, affected by his inspection. "They make you smart. Smart is sexy."

Baxter closed in on her, pressed one hand on the

counter beside her. Inhaling the scent of aroused woman, every muscle in his body tensed with the need he felt for this woman.

"Sexy is you in that dress," he said, a finger trailing the valley between her breasts. He could feel her heart racing beneath his touch, and it pleased him. "Sexier is you out of this dress."

# 6

*SEXIER IS YOU OUT OF this dress.*

Caron cringed as she replayed those words in her mind—Baxter's words—a sudden panic overtaking her. The idea of baring her cleavage had seemed grand, sexy, daring, until she had a realization. When the dress came off, so did the gel bra. Her mind raced. She had to keep the dress on or leave. And judging from her experience with Baxter, if he made any real persuasive effort, she'd be out of this dress.

Intent on escaping, she tried to duck under his arm. He moved, captured her, his big legs pinning hers. His hands palmed her breasts, pushing them together. She looked down, studied her own amazing cleavage in awe and disbelief. If only they were real. His fingers rasped over the bare skin exposed by her skimpy top, the pleasure immense. He felt so damn good, his body, his hands, those lips. She tried to shake off the lusty fog. Desperately, she reached up and covered his hands with hers.

He kissed her, long, deep, and her body warmed. Her hands fell away from his and pressed to his chest, fingers sprawled out in wanton exploration. He was so hard, so strong, so unbelievably wonderful to touch.

Every nerve ending she owned was alive, aware, as his hands slowly traveled over her waist, slid along the curve of her backside. Slowly…as if he were savoring the touch, savoring her. It was amazingly sexy, overwhelmingly hot. He skimmed a path over her ribs before returning to her breasts. He shoved down the lace there, shamelessly exposing her nipples, and tugged them between his fingers before she could object. She moaned into the kiss, forgetting the bra, forgetting everything but how good the touch felt. His gentle touch turned a bit rough, rasping her nipples with calloused fingers and tight little tugs that had her core spasming.

He tore his mouth from hers, leaving her panting for more, as he stared down at the stiff peaks. "Beautiful," he said. "I want to kiss them."

Oh, please, yes. She wet her lips. "O…kay." She squeezed her eyes shut at the ridiculous response. Where was her inner vixen when she needed her? How did anyone play coy when they wanted their nipples kissed?

But he didn't kiss her nipples. Instead, he turned her around, leaned across her body, the hard proof of his arousal nuzzled beneath her backside. He drew down the zipper.

Panic anew arose inside her. She had no idea what to do. "Wait!" His palms slid beneath the open zipper, warm against her midsection, and she pressed into him, the straps of her dress falling down her shoulders.

His hands slid to her stomach as he tugged her gently to him, his lips near her ear. "I can't wait."

She didn't want to wait, either. She didn't want to care about the damn bra. She wished she'd never put it on so she wouldn't be worried about taking it off. Her head fell back against his shoulder. She blinked up at him, distracted by his mouth. Wishing for a taste, for more than a taste. That thought fueled her vixen confidence.

"Prove it," she challenged, asking for what she really wanted. Him naked. How had she gone this long without ripping this man's clothes off? She rotated in his arms to face him, tugged on his shirt. "Take it off," she ordered. "My rules, remember? No clothes for you." Her clit throbbed just thinking about him naked, about him inside her. She was swollen, achy. Wanton in a way she'd never been in her life. And it felt good. So good.

"And you?" he rebutted, the raw desire etched across his features almost enough to make her strip right here and now. Almost. He was going first.

She lifted her chin defiantly. "After you," she said, leaning against the bar to watch him undress, gown now back in place. It was his turn to be a little exposed, and she planned to enjoy every minute.

His pupils darkened, fierce with arousal, rich with a hunger that said he wanted to eat her alive, and she flashed back to the limo, to the intimate way he'd pleasured her, the brazen way she'd writhed in response.

He reached up and loosened his tie, quickly tossing it aside. Next came his shirt. A few buttons undone, then he pulled it over his head, as if he was as impatient as she.

Caron surveyed all that tawny skin, so taut over a spectacular chest sprinkled with dark hair, just begging for her hands. A six-pack of abdominal muscles intended for her mouth. And when, in one easy move, he dropped his pants and underwear, Caron was reminded quite clearly why a gel bra was not a good enough reason to miss this. Not by a long shot, not even close. Baxter was not to be missed.

He stood there, aroused, in all his magnificent, naked glory, all eight inches plus jutting out in front of him, and for the first time in her life, she wanted to go down on her knees. Wanted to. Not because she felt obligated, not because it seemed to be the thing to do. Wanted to take him in her mouth, to lick him up and down. To hear him moan and know she'd made it happen.

He held up a condom. "Care to do the honors." Oh, yeah, she did, and she didn't have to be asked twice. Nerves clamored in her stomach but they were secondary now, her desire to explore this man's body far outreaching any fear of making a fool of herself. Tomorrow this was over. If she let fear win, she'd wake up with regrets.

She pushed off the counter and let the dress slide off her shoulders, suddenly finding it a cumbersome restraint better done away with. That left her with the bra, the hose, the shoes. She'd lost her panties in the limo.

Baxter's hot stare seemed to drink her in with arousing detail. She flushed under the attention, a bit embarrassed, a lot aroused.

Caron went to him then, slid the condom from his hand. She'd never actually put a condom on a man, but she confidently wrapped her hand around his erection, enjoyed the feel of his width in her palm.

Easing to her knees, she touched the pool of liquid hovering on the tip of his swollen head with her tongue.

He moaned, his hips jerking slightly. She smiled, enjoying this power she had over him. Her tongue explored the ridge of his erection before she closed her lips around him. The more she took of him, the more he responded, and the more she wanted him inside more than her mouth. The more her legs spread. The wetter she became. Responding to the needs of her body, Caron tore her mouth from his erection, ripped open the condom and rolled it down his steely length. She'd barely completed the task, when he picked her up and carried her to the couch.

A second later, he was sitting on the couch and she was straddling him, sliding down the long, hard reach of his cock until he was buried deep inside her.

He gently pulled at her wig. "It's falling off," he said. She tried to fix it, and he stopped her. "Get rid of it."

She blinked, not sure what to do. That wig was her persona, the diva who'd allowed her to come there tonight. For just a moment, they sat there, bodies intimately merged, staring at one another. And she felt something in that moment, something intense, something that burned with erotic intensity, yet stripped away the need for emotional inhibition. She neither understood it, nor tried. It simply released her to freedom, pleasure.

Caron reached up and loosened the pins holding the wig, and tossed it onto the couch. Baxter pulled the clip holding her own hair on top of her head. She shook it out.

"I like you like this," he said, twining his fingers in her hair and joining his lips to hers.

She didn't know if he meant the words, didn't even have time to consider the unveiling of Caron, the destruction of Marilyn. Because this was a kiss like none he had given her to this point, a kiss that consumed, as if he literally breathed her in, as if they were merging, becoming one. She felt him thicken inside her, felt the pulse of his arousal. Felt the first thrust of his hips as they began to sway together, rocking with a slow, sultry rhythm. They devoured one another, drank of one another, absorbed one another.

Somewhere along the line, she lost her bra and she didn't care. He stared at her breasts as if they were beautiful, touched them with hot, needy hands. Caron forgot Marilyn, she forgot fear. She moved sensually with passion, with the ultimate hunt for that place of no return—where she exploded in a rush of frenzied action and clung to him as he shook with his own release.

Long minutes later, she buried her face in his shoulder, satisfied, reconnecting with herself. Which was when she started worrying about what came next.

As if he sensed her unease, Baxter stole her moment of fear, framing her face with his hands as he studied her. "Do you remember what you called that orgasm I gave you in the limousine?"

Her brows dipped. Was this a trick question? "Nice?"

His expression darkened. "That's what I was afraid of. We have more work to do." He stood up, her body still wrapped around his.

"What?" she asked. "Where are we going?"

"To the bedroom," he said, holding her as if she were featherlight. "I told you I was going to make you come until you forget that word, and I meant it."

Caron laughed in disbelief. This might be a long night, because she wasn't giving up on the word *nice* until she was darn good and ready.

CARON LAY NUZZLED UNDER Baxter's shoulder, her hand on his chest as he slept. She stared across the room, through the open patio window, to the moon hovering low, threatening to be replaced by sunlight. She couldn't sleep, and she didn't want to wake up to be stuffed into an awkward Marilyn costume, trying to navigate an equally awkward morning-after. The question was— how did she get out of here without Baxter waking up? And what to do when she did? She had no purse, no money. Considering she had to leave dressed as Marilyn, the sooner the better. She didn't need unwanted attention. Flexing her fingers on his chest, Caron inhaled one last breath of Baxter's scrumptious male scent, and then gently eased away from him. Or tried.

He lifted his head, tightened his arm around her. "Where are you going?"

"Bathroom," she murmured.

"Hurry back," he replied sleepily, patting her on the ass.

Caron's heart fluttered. He liked her ass, he'd made that clear. She'd liked that he liked it. But it was done, over. Baxter appeared unworried about an awkward morning-after. He was Baxter Remington, and even Caron, reader of romance, not newspapers, knew his reputation. A new woman every time he was photographed. Maybe he was just so used to morning-afters, they weren't weird to him anymore.

Caron scooted off the bed, naked, aware of feeling exposed for the first time in hours. Sadness pitted in her stomach. Her Cinderella night was over. She tiptoed toward the bedroom door, ignoring the bathroom, though she could darn sure use a little detour in that direction. Looked as if she'd be squeezing her legs closed upon exiting Baxter's apartment just as she had entered, but this time the reason wouldn't be quite so joyful.

She snagged her shoes on departure, one by the bed, one by the door—not sure how that had happened. The thigh-highs, she wasn't even going to try to find. Quietly, she rounded up her clothes and dressed, leaving the wig on the couch. The sexy dress was enough zing and bling to draw watchful gazes on its own—she didn't need the blonde Marilyn thing going on along with it.

Dressed but for the shoes—which she planned to carry for the sake of quietness—she began the hunt for a pen, to leave a note. It seemed wrong not to. Problem was, the apartment was so darn neat, free of any signs of real living, let alone anything useful, like that pen.

A snakelike, steel stairwell in the far corner of the room led to a loftlike area above. Why hadn't she noticed that before? Right. Why? She knew why. Because all she'd cared about last night was Baxter's naked body. She frowned. Was it an office? Yes. It looked like an office.

Shoes dangling from her fingers, she tiptoed up the stairwell and then stood in awe at what she found. It was a library. A library! Full of books. Fiction, history, business. Big fluffy chairs with lamps and tables beside them. Windows offering a dreamy view. It was the most wonderful room. A room she had always longed to have in her own home. And she'd accused him of having no books. Who would have thought? She sighed. She liked Baxter. Too much. His playfulness. The way he made her laugh and forget nerves and inhibitions. Regret curled inside her at never seeing him again, and she shook herself. She had to get moving.

Her bare feet sank into plush carpeting as she moved to the corner desk by the window and found a pen and paper. She studied the blank page, unsure what to say, but certain she was out of time. Baxter would discover her absence soon. A mischievous smile slid onto her lips and she started scribbling. "Thanks for a 'nice' night." Pleased with herself, she retopped the pen and set it down.

She rushed to the stairs and hurried back to the lower level, thankful all was still peaceful there. In a quick dart, she made it to the door and exited, sticking the piece of paper in the door. Now, to creatively figure out how to pay for a cab with no wallet. This should be interesting.

After twenty minutes of trying, and the early-morning sky blossoming with oranges and yellows, Caron accepted she wasn't getting a cab with the promise of payment on the other end of the ride, and she simply wasn't willing to charge Baxter's account. So she started walking, the breeze from the nearby water turning sixty degrees into fifty. And she had no coat and a slinky dress on. Thankfully she was in a good area of town, and the sun was fast rising. It was an idea that lasted a block. She was freezing. She had to go back, to charge Baxter's account. She'd send him the money later that day. She turned to retreat and found a petite blonde approaching in slim black jeans and a turtleneck, a businesslike look on her chiseled face.

"Caron Avery?"

A badge flashed in front of Caron and she frowned. "FBI?"

"Agent Sarah Walker. You are Caron Avery, correct?"

"I am," Caron agreed cautiously. "Did I do something wrong?" Concern prickled. "Oh, God. Is something wrong at my store? Was I robbed?"

"Your store is fine, Ms. Avery," she quickly assured, though her tone was serious. "I'm here about Baxter Remington." A dark sedan pulled up beside them. "Why don't you let us give you a ride home, Ms. Avery, and I'll explain?"

Alarm bells went off in her head. "I'm all about respecting the law, Ms...."

"Agent Walker."

"Agent Walker," Caron amended, hugging herself against the chilly air that darn near had her teeth chattering. "But I'm not getting into a car with you just because you flash a badge. How do I know it's real?"

The woman raised a brow in surprise before a look of appreciation settled on it. Several cabs pulled up to the red light at the corner, and Agent Walker rushed to the edge of the sidewalk, signaling for one's attention. One of the cabs backed up and parked in front of the sedan.

Agent Walker yanked open the back door and called to Caron. "I'll spring for the ride to your apartment."

Caron's indecision lasted all of ten seconds before she dashed toward the cab. She was too cold to turn down a cab, and it seemed as safe, or safer, than walking. In the backseat of the car, Caron tried to subdue her shivers, offering the driver her address.

Agent Walker was quick to join her, wasting no time getting to her point. "We need your help, Ms. Avery." Her voice was low, for Caron's ears only. "Baxter Remington's partner is being investigated for securities fraud and he's gone MIA. He has ties to a certain investor who miraculously knew the exact moment to unload his Remington stock. We believe Baxter knows where his partner is."

Now she understood what Baxter meant by scandal, and why he'd wanted to protect her from the press. It appeared that the FBI wasn't so easily avoided. "Maybe he doesn't know anything. And what does that have to do with me?"

"We need you to use whatever bond you have with Baxter to find out exactly what he does know."

A disbelieving laugh bubbled from Caron's lips. "Me?" she asked. "I have nothing to do with Baxter Remington. You've got the wrong girl."

"Weren't you with him tonight?"

"That has nothing—"

"Then you're the right girl. You can do this. You *have* to do this. It's your duty as a citizen to use the opportunity you have to get close to this man and stop any wrongdoing."

Okay, now Caron was getting mad. "Duty?" she asked. "How is it my duty when I don't even know this man?"

"Then why are you leaving his apartment at the crack of dawn?"

Caron opened her mouth and shut it. Bit her tongue and processed, flustered. This was none of their business. "I won't be seeing him again," she finally ground out. "Period. End of story. No forwarding number or address left."

"It's your duty as a good citizen to see him again. You have a chance to stop someone from getting away with a crime."

Caron shook the cobwebs from her head. "Let me get this straight. Baxter isn't being accused of wrongdoing, but you want me to manipulate him to catch someone who is? And you're calling that my duty?"

"We don't know what Mr. Remington's role in all of this is, but aiding and abetting a wanted man is a felony, Ms. Avery. So yes, Mr. Remington could very well be in a great deal of trouble."

"But all you want to do is question Baxter's partner," she pointed out. "He's not charged with a crime. I don't know the law all that well, yet that does seem relevant."

"He'll be charged," the agent assured her. "And so will your lover boy is he's not careful."

Anger began to curl in Caron's belly at what was nothing more than a manipulative threat. "Clearly, you have no proof Baxter knows where his partner is. I mean, surely you've done your surveillance on him and found nothing damning or you wouldn't be talking to me right now." She gave a little snort. "Because I have to tell you that thinking I can get answers from Baxter Remington is putting you in the pretty desperate category. As I told you." The cab pulled up to Caron's building, and she quickly opened the door. "I can't help you, Agent Walker."

"Can't or won't?"

"Both," Caron stated, and tried to get out of the cab. She'd always had instincts about people, and Baxter wasn't a felon. A bit arrogant, a lot playboy, but not a felon. She wouldn't be party to manipulating innocent people. Not that she had any influence over Baxter in the first place.

Agent Walker gently shackled her arm. "You can do this. I saw the way he looked at you at that party. You have his attention."

"You saw the way he looked at a dolled-up fantasy. That's not me."

Agent Walker seemed as if she would insist further, but she didn't. She dropped her hold on Caron. "Think about it, Ms. Avery. I'll be in touch."

Caron climbed out of the car, and it sped away. She turned and looked at her building and cringed. She didn't have her keys. They were in her purse. It seemed her fantasy night had started with the toilet and ended there, too. Maybe she should have stayed for that awkward morning-after. A hunk of a hot man and a warm bed sounded pretty darn "nice" right now.

# 7

MONDAY MORNING BAXTER stood at the window of the conference room. His weekend rendezvous with Marilyn was not forgotten, but the day had started with the grim depiction of Remington Coffee's tumbling stocks. He now listened to a group of five employees as they debated "image management" and ways to increase sales, while the PR person he'd hired, Katie Kelley, nixed one idea after the other.

Baxter scanned the oceanfront horizon. Doing so reminded him of how he'd spent far too much time this weekend staring at that damn note Caron had left him. Her message "thanks for a 'nice' night" had taunted him. It wasn't like him to be so easily distracted, and certainly not in the midst of a crisis, but he couldn't stop the burn to want to find Caron and prove how much better than "nice" their night had been. But he'd restrained himself. This unfamiliar need to prove something to a woman served no purpose, and would most certainly drag her into his present hell. But that hadn't stopped him from sending Caron a little goodbye of his own by way of his assistant, to arrive at her bookstore this morning.

"What do you think, Mr. Remington?" Katie asked,

referring to a suggestion for a "Remington for Kids" fun time at select coffee shops every weekend. A portion of all sales during the event would be donated to charity. "With Christmas only a few short weeks away, we could use the holiday as a launching platform. The program will appear motivated by the holiday, not the scandal."

Baxter turned to the group sitting around the rectangular mahogany table and dismissed the idea. "We've never made our charity events self-serving."

"It's well-timed charity, Mr. Baxter," Katie countered. "The public needs something to talk about other than the scandal. Because speaking frankly, there is a natural human tendency to cling to the scandalous."

Reluctantly, Baxter agreed. And a vice president accused of insider trading, now gone missing, was pretty scandalous. And damning where investors were concerned.

She continued, "We must counteract the negative media attention, flood the memory banks with positive. And remember that staying strong in their eyes allows you to continue to give back in such a generous way while securing your employees' futures, as well."

Baxter felt a steely punch in his gut for the people Jett had put in jeopardy, guilty or not, by fleeing. Everything his father, his family, had built was in jeopardy.

"I find your points valid, Ms. Kelley," he conceded. "However, there are those who will spin whatever we do into something corrupt right now. We must tread carefully." Strategic, rapid action—that's what his father had preached and what Baxter lived.

"If I may," offered Dan Moore, VP of marketing,

clearing his throat. He was thirty-something, ambitious, full of good ideas with action to back them up. "Why not roll out a program that's threefold and appeals to more than one type of consumer." He ticked the three areas off on his fingers. "Discounts, charity, new product."

The debate continued for another hour until Baxter finally found a comfort level and agreed to the three-pronged approach, sending Katie, Dan and the rest of his staff on their way to make it all happen—preferably yesterday. Finding his way back to his office, he passed in front of his secretary's desk as she juggled a delivery person and several phone calls.

At sixty, Lorraine had been with his father before working for him. Not only slender and elegant, she had enough style and snap to teach a few of the much younger up-and-comers around the office the meaning of the word *professional*. Baxter couldn't live without her.

He'd barely settled behind his desk when Lorraine poked her head in his office.

"How are you holding up?"

He waved her forward. "Better than I would be without you," he countered, not as a compliment, but the simple truth.

Lorraine shut the door behind her and then perched on the edge of the chair in front of his desk, pad of paper and messages in hand. "Your father called from Europe. He's—"

"Worried," Baxter said, as he pressed his fingers to the bridge of his nose and then let go. "I know. And let me guess. My mother called. She's worried."

"And wants to remind you about your sister's thirty-fifth birthday on Saturday. You're headed out of town for the rest of the week. It's likely to be busy when you return. I thought you might want me to pick up a gift."

"No," he said. "I'll go today." Maybe he'd go to Caron's store and look for a gift. But he left that part out, adding, "Thirty-five is a big birthday. I want it to be special." He and Becky were only two years apart, him being the oldest; they'd grown up close and remained that way. He wanted her gift to be special. "Remind me again why I thought this Texas trip was a good idea?"

"You wanted to be sure the new stores meet company standards and rally the troops," she answered, as if he didn't know his own reasons. "Why not cancel?"

He nixed that as quickly as Katie had rejected a dozen ideas. "A cancellation might rattle the staff. I don't want them thinking that trouble is keeping me away."

"Well, there is one positive to an absence," she commented. "The FBI can't camp on your doorstep." She slid a pile of messages to his desk. "The top three are all from Agent Sarah Walker, who would like you to call her, apparently right away since she won't stop calling."

He scrubbed his jaw. "What else?"

"Confirmation the package you wanted delivered was received," she said, setting the slip on his desk, showing that the courier had, indeed, left Caron his little package.

"Oh, my," Lorraine laughed. "I wish I'd looked inside that package. I'd like to know what put that expression on your face."

Baxter blinked. "I have no idea what you're talking about."

"I've known you since you were a kid, Baxter Remington," she scolded. "I know a look when I see one."

Having no intention of opening the door to speculation, he pushed to his feet. He didn't know why Caron wouldn't get out of his head, but it was time to find out. "I'll grab that gift before my next series of meetings begins."

Lorraine stood, as well. "Did I mention you don't need to call back that FBI agent?"

His brow lifted and she continued, "She's in the lobby waiting for you." She shrugged. "I figured as many of these meetings as you've endured, she could wait until we were done."

Baxter would have laughed at Lorraine's tactics if it wasn't for the dread he had of yet another FBI meeting. He'd been cooperative above and beyond what his attorney had advised.

"I'll tell her goodbye on my way out the door," he quipped, crossing the room. He exited to the lobby.

A petite blonde sprang to her feet from a lobby chair, and Baxter barely spared her a glance. He punched the elevator button as she rushed to his side.

"If you have something to ask me, do it on the ride down," he scolded, punching the elevator button again.

"I'd think you'd prefer these matters private," the woman said, reaching his side.

The familiar female voice grated a nerve. Baxter knew her. The woman from the party, the one he'd suspected of being with the press. He sliced her a chilling look. "Do you often try and seduce the men you're trying to question?"

"I don't remember ever being given the chance to

identify myself," she countered. "We need answers, Mr. Remington."

He shook his head. The elevator opened and he walked inside, hovering in the doorway to block her entry. "On second thought," he told her, "I'll take this ride down on my own. Call my attorney. I think he'll have a word or two more to say this time." He stepped back inside the car and let the door shut.

He realized then one of the reasons why Caron appealed so much to him. Even in that Marilyn Monroe costume, she'd been real, one-hundred-percent pure honesty. One of the few people he'd met who was so purely human, flaws and opinions, and personality. No games that weren't shared fun.

She was a breath of fresh air in the midst of secrets and lies. And he couldn't seem to fight the urge to see her just one more time. Besides, who was he kidding? He knew he was going to see her when he'd sent that package. That note she'd left him had all but been a challenge—and he'd never been one to walk away from a challenge.

APPARENTLY BEING MARILYN came with more perks than just Baxter Remington for a night. By midmorning Monday, The Book Nook had not only debuted its new romance loft, but done so with a rush of Christmas shoppers.

Things were so crazy that, in a panic, Kasey had called her roommate, Alice, to ask her to come in and run the register. And though Caron didn't fool herself into thinking things would remain this busy—after all, there had been coupons and special deals announced at the charity event—even a small portion of this traffic would do a world of good toward paying back her grandmother.

Standing behind the front counter, half supervising Alice, Caron finished preparing the "Romance in a Bag" special advertised at the charity show, which included a candle, a bookmark, a pen and a book of choice from the loft. Alice wished a customer a good day and seemed to be doing well. Kasey had the other customers handled. Things were finally calming down. Caron finished arranging the display she had set up by the front door with the Romance bags, and then started for her office.

"Oh, wait!" Alice called out. "This came for you a few minutes ago."

Caron frowned and accepted the shoe-box-sized delivery with no return address, wondering at the funny flutter in her stomach that seemed some sort of premonition. Brushing off the feeling, she weighed the package with her hands—it was light, maybe the silk scarves she'd ordered.

A few moments later, she sat at her desk, the flutter in her stomach back again as she cut open the box. Tissue paper covered the contents; a note card sat on top of the paper. She flipped open the card, a few slashes of masculine writing on the simple white page.

You never know when you might find an occasion to wear it again. But I kept the panties. I didn't get a goodbye. You owed me a keepsake.

There was no signature.

Caron lifted the tissue and then shoved it back

down, her heart thundering against her rib cage. It was her wig. Oh, God. Baxter had sent her the wig. And kept her *panties!* She reread the note; her heart raced some more—as erratically as three drums playing to different tunes. *You never know when you might find an occasion to wear it again.* As in, with him? No. That was insane. She was so not his kind of woman. He was not her kind of guy, not that she really knew what kind of guy *was* her kind of guy. But not Baxter. Not a filthy rich playboy who controlled everyone and everything around him. He'd sure controlled her. And well…that had been rather pleasurable, but just for a night. A fizzle of excitement lifted the corners of her lips. Of course, she'd done a good deal of controlling, too. And making that man moan had been so erotic.

"The toilet is stopped up again," Kasey announced, appearing in Caron's office doorway and blasting away her fantasy with a hard knock of bitter reality. "I sealed the door and, ah, well, sprayed some of the perfume samples."

Caron slammed the box top shut, taking in the announcement with painful disbelief. "Oh, please, no," Caron said, her hand pressing to her rolling stomach. "Not today." The bathroom was in the romance loft, of all places.

Kasey gave a stop-sign motion with her hands. "Before you freak out," she said, "I called the plumber and screamed, so *you* don't have to. He said he'd be here in thirty minutes and that was fifteen minutes ago. It took me that long to get away from a customer to come tell you. And as much as I hate to show this to you," she said, she set a piece of paper on the desk, "you need to see it before he gets here."

Caron studied the plumber's bill from Friday night and about fell over. "Five hundred dollars!" she exclaimed. "Is he *insane?* And it's broken again on top of that?"

Kasey nodded, her expression saying she knew the plumber was going to be sorry for both—the bill and the broken toilet.

"There are people everywhere," came the blurted announcement from Alice as she appeared in the doorway. "I need help." She lowered her voice, "And, oh, my God, there is this really hot guy who just came in and all the women are panting. Me included." She disappeared again.

Kasey cleared her throat. "Sounds like the situation requires attention." She disappeared.

On another occasion, recognizing that Kasey's urgency translated to "I really have to go see this guy, if he's that hot," Caron might have laughed at the youthful folly. As for Caron, there were only two men on her mind right now and both had her in knots. The plumber who had her pipes clogged and her temper hot. And Baxter, who also had her hot, but in a totally different way.

She grabbed the box and held it over the trash can, telling herself to stop thinking about the man, but she couldn't make herself drop the package. With a heavy sigh, she shoved the box under her desk. She should return the wig to the costume shop, as Betsy had requested when Caron had picked up her purse and dropped off the dress. She bit her lip. Or just pay for the wig. Make it her keepsake, as Baxter did her panties.

She squeezed her eyes shut. He had her *panties*. It means nothing, she told herself. He was just paying her back for her little "nice" note, which had clearly been a mistake. No doubt, a man such as Baxter had to end things on his terms. Which really irritated her because part of what had made that night so spectacular was the way he'd shared the power, the way he'd made her laugh, and feel as if they were sharing more than their bodies.

Power plays didn't sit well with Caron, and this felt like that to her. His way of making it clear who had seduced who. Her note had been a joke, a funny memory of their night together. And damn it, he didn't seduce her. She'd seduced him. Or maybe they'd seduced each other. She grimaced. *This* was why she kept to the real world, her fantasies between the pages of books. "Except for Friday night," she whispered.

"He's here!" Kasey yelled from down the hall. "He's here, Caron!"

Caron rounded her desk, ready for a battle. She charged down the hall and cut a fast right to the stairwell, her focus onefold now—the plumber and his ridiculous bill were getting a whack of her attention. She exploded on him in the bathroom to find him packing up his bag to leave.

"It's fixed?" she demanded, bringing into view the same cranky fifty-something plumber from Friday night. He shot her an irritated look that said he wasn't answering a stupid question. Picking up his bag, he casually tossed it over one shoulder. "Wait!" she demanded, walking to the edge of the toilet to inspect his work. "For real, this time?"

"Old pipes, lady," he said. "Replace the entire system or use this." He handed her a plunger and another bill. "That'll save you some money next time." He started walking toward the door.

Caron gaped down at the invoice for two hundred dollars and whirled in pursuit, but stopped dead in her tracks to avoid running into the man now blocking the exit.

"Baxter?" she whispered, shocked to find him here, looking every bit as scrumptious in a dark suit as he had in a tuxedo.

Amusement danced in his dark eyes as he glanced at the plunger in her hand before returning his gaze to her face. "Problem?"

Heat rushed to Caron's cheeks as she realized how far from her Friday-night fantasy she must look— brown hair twisted neatly at the back of her head, a prim black suit, and well, the damn plunger in her hand.

She shook off the embarrassment. Unwilling to let the plumber escape, she thrust the plunger at Baxter. "Hold this," she said and started forward but rethought her rash rudeness. "Please. And thank you." With an inhaled breath, and no time to lose, she squeezed past Baxter, an instant charge darting through her body.

Caron rushed down the stairs, liquid fire shimmering through her limbs, memories of intimate, shared moments with Baxter fluttering through her mind, of being naked and entwined. She couldn't believe he was here, in her store, and instead of challenging him over the meaning of that package he'd sent, she was chasing after the plumber. She had to deal with one man and his mischief at a time. But Baxter's turn was coming.

# 8

BAXTER STOOD IN THAT BATHROOM doorway and shook his head, a low chuckle sliding from his lips. Never in his life would he have imagined his efforts to seduce a woman would result in him holding a toilet plunger, nor would he have ever believed he would actually find himself in pursuit of the woman who'd given it to him.

Disposing of the plunger, Baxter followed in Caron's wake as she pursued the plumber, a path that took him to a hallway leading to a back door.

"I am not paying seven hundred dollars for a plunger!" she hollered to the back of the guy's head as the back door slammed shut.

Caron threw her hands up in the air and then pressed her hand to her face, turning to blink Baxter into focus. "Oh," she said. "I'm sorry. I—it's just that…I'm having plumbing problems."

"I remember that from Friday night," he offered, biting back a smile.

She frowned, a cute dimple forming between her brows. "Friday night? I don't remember telling you about my plumbing problems. No. I didn't. I wouldn't do that."

Did she really think he didn't remember her from the

front door of the hotel? "You told the doorman." He lowered his voice, though the hallway curved away from the store, away from the ears and eyes of potential eavesdroppers. "I liked the pink sweat suit almost as much as the dress. I didn't go looking for Marilyn. Or for Audrey. I went looking for the woman in that pink sweat suit."

She looked surprised, her gaze shifting to the store—ensuring they weren't being overheard, he assumed. Then, "I didn't know you knew that was me. I..." She stopped, sealed her lips. Then, drew herself up straight. "Why are you here?" she demanded.

He laughed. There was the Caron he'd found so adorable—equally flustered, direct and to the point. It was her way of hiding vulnerability but it didn't work. Not with him.

"I need a birthday gift for my sister. Kasey seemed to believe you could help. She said you have a knack for picking the perfect gifts."

She looked as if she might refuse, but Kasey quickly nixed that idea by appearing.

"Oh, good," she said to Caron. "He found you. I told him you'd have a better idea than me about a gift for his sister." She glanced at Baxter. "Again, I'm sorry I wasn't more help. It's crazy busy, and Caron is better at picking gifts than me anyway. I don't want to steer you wrong for such an important occasion." She glanced at Caron. "It's his sister's thirty-fifth birthday. She likes to travel, and she considers herself an amateur chef, right?"

"Thank you, Kasey," he said, offering a nod, and Kasey's face filled with a schoolgirl flush, before she quickly excused herself.

Baxter fixed Caron with an expectant look, his brow arched. "So?" he asked. "Will you come to the rescue and help me find the perfect gift?"

CARON LOST HERSELF in Baxter's dark, probing stare—a stare that intimately stroked her into such a frenzy of awareness that she wanted to run away. Or run to him. Maybe bury her nose in his jacket for just a tiny minute and inhale that delicious spicy scent of his. A dangerous proposition that said she needed to expedite his departure before she went and did something like sleep with the man again. He didn't want her. She didn't care if he claimed he wanted the girl in the pink sweats—he'd been enthralled with the fantasy. Now he wanted the fantasy woman in the wig and a chance to end things on his terms. She wanted no part of being used. The man had her panties; he wasn't getting anything else. She had to take this situation and get it under control. Put him in his place, not the opposite, which she was certain was his intention.

"You came for a gift," she said flatly, her disbelief meant to be obvious.

His eyes held mischief and mayhem, proving he was not at all affected by her directness. A sound rich and masculine, escaped his lips—lips she knew to be firm but gentle.

"I really *do* need a gift," he said, his hands held up in defense. "My sister's birthday is Saturday, and I'm headed out of town tomorrow for the rest of the week."

"Don't you have an assistant who does that sort of thing for you?"

He gave her a knowing look—as if he knew she was

trying to turn him into the bad guy. And she was. If he were the bad guy, then ignoring his hot body and charming smile would be oh-so-much easier. "I'd never allow anyone else to pick out a gift for my sister."

She wasn't letting him off that easily. Tilting her chin up, she fixed him in a steady stare and walked toward him, pausing next to him. "So, just by coincidence, you happened to end up in my store to buy it."

"No coincidence," he promised in a low, velvety voice. "I came here for you, Caron."

Caron's breath hitched in her throat at that announcement, her body betraying her decision to resist. *I came here for you, Caron.* No. She rejected that claim. He came for a game of cat and mouse, and control. A game she feared would only end badly. She liked Baxter, liked him far too much to delve any deeper into this thing, this whatever it was, going on between them. She'd get hurt. He'd simply walk away without a glance back.

She opened her mouth to tell him in no uncertain terms she wasn't interested, but found herself cut short when Alice's voice cut through the air.

"Caron! Kasey! Someone. Help, please!"

Caron inhaled and turned to find her new helper struggling with the cash register, which was known for jamming, while three customers patiently waited to check out.

"She's new," Caron murmured to Baxter, more than a little happy for a quick retreat to gain some composure. "I'll be right back."

She scurried away, aware of every step taken under his watchful regard. Her skin prickled. A few punched keys, and Alice was set. Kasey appeared, as well, with a customer in tow, her eyes alight with as much mischief as Baxter's. Mischief that said she'd intention- ally brought Baxter to Caron—no doubt, playing matchmaker. Little did Kasey know, the match had been made, and with a blonde bombshell packing a gel bra—a temporary persona that was apparently more successful with the opposite sex than the real her. That costume had empowered her and allowed her to escape her inhibitions, even when it had been discarded. Morning had come and she'd gone back to her simple reality where her seduction prowess was a big whopping zero. That realization sat uncomfortably. She knew she had to deal with Baxter and be done with this.

Caron found Baxter patiently leaning against a wall, still watching her—inspecting her with an attentive, heavy-lidded stare that explained the heated flush of her skin that refused to cool.

"This way," she said, motioning to the back of the store, where bookshelves lined walls and came together in a far too secluded corner. A narrow, round table sat in the center of the snug aisle to allow customers to sit and study their potential purchases. And though privacy with a man like Baxter could easily prove dangerous to a girl's willpower, Caron decided it had its merits right about now, offering a chance for confrontation.

The instant they were out of sight of the rest of the store, Caron whirled around to confront Baxter. She found him closer than expected. So close. Too close.

"Why are you really here?" she demanded, intend- ing to get the obvious out in the open and, therefore, end this awkward torture of the unspoken between them.

"I needed a gift. I *wanted* to see you." His attention flickered over her lips, before he prodded, "Aren't you even a little pleased to see me?"

No. Yes. She was. She didn't want to be but she was. That was why she wasn't about to answer that question, "This is about my note, isn't it? You took it as some kind of challenge."

The air crackled with instant challenge. "Was it?"

"No!" she hissed in a whisper, his question telling her that he did, indeed, see it as a challenge. This was not about her, but his male ego. "It was a joke. Over. Done with. A way to say goodbye." Wasn't it? Had she subconsciously wanted to challenge him? No! She shook off that idea, refusing to analyze herself.

Find the gift and get some distance, she told herself. She redirected the conversation. "Kasey said your sister loves to travel and cook?"

He didn't immediately answer, his expression indecipherable but for a tiny hint of calculation ticking away in his dark eyes. Then finally, his expression shifted, softened, and he said, "She's a high school teacher, world history, and world culture is her obsession. She thinks experiencing that culture makes her a better teacher. That includes learning about the food and trying to re-create it for her classes. Right now, Russia is her obsession. I thought maybe something that would feed that interest."

There was genuine thoughtfulness behind his words, in his expression. He really needed a gift, she admitted, and not only that, he cared about making it special for his sister. "I think that's a wonderful idea."

"I'm probably too late for this, but I don't suppose you would have a cookbook that has Russian cuisine?"

"No," she said. "Typically, smaller stores don't stock something so customized to a small niche market, especially with the Internet so readily accessible."

He grimaced. "I should have planned ahead. I don't want to show up with some generic, meaningless gift."

She thought of the FBI agents, and noted Baxter had his own little "plumbing" problems going on. She considered telling him about the agent who'd approached her but decided it might be better left alone.

"No worries," she replied, sympathizing with the hell he must be going through. "I can special order something that will fit the bill and have it delivered to wherever you'd like in time for her birthday. But," Caron said, and held up a finger, "I have an idea." She bent down to the bottom row of a shelf and removed a large, glossy book.

Baxter stood above her, his hand gliding down one of the shelves. "You have a unique selection of books. Travel. History. A little of everything."

"I try to carry unique, special choices in every genre since I can't carry the variety that a bigger store can." She pushed to her feet, the heaviness of the oversize book a bit of a struggle. Baxter clearly noticed as much, reaching out to offer aid. Their hands collided; electricity darted up her arm, her eyes riveting on his. "Thank you," she whispered, allowing him to fully take the weight from her and set the book on the table.

Their eyes held, a magnetic pull of awareness, of memories of intimate touches shared. A connection that made her heart flutter and chest tighten. A connection that made her forget the wig and the costume, and remember the sultry touches and mind-drugging kisses.

He reached out and plucked a wayward strand of her hair. "Do you know how badly I want to pull those pins free and then kiss you?"

She reached up and swiped the hair out of his reach. "Behave," she whispered.

A low rumble of laughter escaped his lips. "But you like it when I misbehave."

"You're trying to get a reaction," she said, calling him on his motive. "And we both know it."

"Is it working?"

"Yes," she answered. "So stop."

He leaned against the bookshelf. "Are you always so direct?"

"You have a problem with direct?" she countered.

"I prefer it," he said and motioned toward the book. "So tell me why you chose this one." He straightened to study her selection.

Caron ran her hand over the gorgeous collage of exotic locations on the cover. "Besides being a gorgeous display piece for her home, it features an array of wonderful travel locations with pictorials and recipes for each region." She turned it around to offer him a chance to glance through it, watching as he studied the selection.

"It's perfect," he said, flipping through a few pages with a satisfied look on his face. "She'll love it. Is there time to order that cookbook, as well?"

"Of course," she said. "I can e-mail you some choices and let you pick."

"From what I've seen, I'm safe trusting you. Especially since I'll be traveling." He turned and scanned a wall of rare history books with approval. "Once my sister finds your store—and she will—once she opens her gift, she'll spend hours here. And most likely you'll end up with her entire class visiting with her one day."

"We'd be thrilled to have her class," Caron said, pleased by the sincerity she sensed in him. She'd put a lot of heart and soul into the store, and she was proud of it. "I'll order the cookbook today and then have everything wrapped and delivered by Friday to whatever address you leave."

"My home," he said. "I won't be back till Friday night. The front desk will hold the packages for me."

His home. Where they'd made love too many times to count. She cleared her throat, straightened. "Let me jot down that address in my office."

She reached for the book.

He snagged it first. "I'll carry it."

She gave a quick nod and passed him, leading him to her office, but not without a quick pause to accept praise from a customer who adored the new romance loft. Baxter waited patiently and then cast her an interested look as the fifty-something woman rushed to the register to make her purchase. Caron motioned him toward the hall and her office.

"You're a hit," he commented. "All you need now is a Remington coffee shop inside the store."

She laughed. "Is that right?"

"Everything's better with a cup of Remington coffee," he teased. "Didn't you know that?"

"Way too extravagant for my budget," she said quickly and then blushed, pausing in front of her office door. "Oh, no." She waved a hand. Once again she was insulting the prices of his coffee without meaning to. "That came out wrong. I didn't mean your coffee was too extravagant. I mean having a coffee bar in the store is."

His lips twitched. "That's not what you said the other night," he reminded her.

Heat slid up her neck. "That doesn't mean I don't like it," she quickly inserted. The truth was, she'd often dreamed of having a coffee shop in the store, but it was simply too costly an endeavor to consider.

Eager to change the subject, she motioned him inside her office, and she quickly darted behind the protective shield of her simple wooden desk. It was a tiny office, made smaller by his dominating presence, and no doubt, no comparison to his executive-flavored world or expensive leather furnishings. There was no brass and glass, no money dripping from the walls. Just bookshelves much like those lining the walls of the store, with her personal collection of books and knickknacks.

She slid a piece of paper and a pen across the wooden surface of her desk. "If you can jot down that address. I can include the bill in the package if you like?"

"That would be excellent," he said agreeably, and then with easy male grace, crossed the small distance between the door and her desk. He reached for the paper and pen, scribbled his address with that powerful male writing of his and then looked up at her. "And please include a gift certificate for a hundred dollars."

His cell phone buzzed and he glanced down at the screen, a furrow forming in his brow. "Business never stops." He slid the note toward her. "The first address is for the package." His eyes darkened, turned intimate, as did his voice. The room seemed to shrink even smaller. "The second address is the private dinner club I'll be at tonight. Ten o'clock. Alone."

He gave her no time to respond. Turning away, he sauntered toward the door, his casual composure holding her as spellbound as the invitation, free of the demand for an immediate answer, free of pressure, and she was glad for it. He'd handed her the power as he had many times Friday night. But Caron wasn't sure she knew how to deal with him outside of the freedom of the glitz, glamour and costumes.

"I thought you were worried about the press?" she called to him, reaching for anything that might convince her to walk away from this before she did something silly, like fall for Baxter Remington instead of simply falling into bed with him.

He turned and winked. "That's what the wig is for," he said, and then departed, leaving Caron with an office filled with his spicy male cologne and temptation.

He wanted her to wear the wig. Caron stared after him, wrestling with a kaleidoscope of emotions. He'd given her back the power of the costume, the veil of a seductress. Why did that bother her so much?

CARON SAT IN THE BACK of a Yellow Cab on the way to the address Baxter had left her and pressed her fingers to her mouth. Coming here had been a tormenting choice. But ultimately, Friday night's lovemaking was still so vivid, she could almost taste Baxter on her lips. Depriving herself of such pleasure seemed ridiculous. She was a grown woman with needs and desires. A woman who deserved to have those needs fulfilled. And Baxter had proven he knew how to deliver—why go elsewhere? Besides, she'd worn the wig, like a veil, or a shield… Yes, a shield. A shield that allowed her to explore her sexuality, let her be the seductress of Friday night. She hoped.

The driver pulled the car to a stop in front of a corner lot, a fancy brick building with valet parking and doormen—her destination. Caron paid the driver, and then drew a deep breath, before opening the car door. She slid out, tugging at the black skirt that rode just above the knee. She wore a sheer black silk blouse and knee-high boots. She'd added a velvet blazer for warmth, which she tugged more snuggly around her, the wind whipping as fiercely as her stomach rolled. The wind calmed a moment later; her stomach did not.

She approached the doormen, found herself dropping Baxter's name—her…dropping names. This was insane. So not her world. But sure as she said his name, she was swept inside, treated like a princess. She liked it, too. She didn't want to like it. Why start liking something you couldn't have? Live the fantasy, Caron, she told herself. But she'd never been good at the whole window-shopping kind of thing. If she couldn't have something, why taunt herself?

Dim lights and elegance greeted her, the entry adorned with a gorgeous crystal chandelier dangling above a mahogany table. And the red and white floral arrangement, the largest that Caron had ever seen, sat as a centerpiece—fake no doubt. No one could afford to have that many flowers delivered every day. Or maybe they could, but Caron didn't even want to think about the price tag. And that only proved how out of her element she truly was. She couldn't enjoy the decor without thinking about how much it cost.

A man in his late forties appeared in front of her, his salt-and-pepper hair sleek and perfectly groomed. He wore a tuxedo and waved her toward the stairs. "This way, miss."

Caron followed him up a marble stairway lined with an Oriental rug in a delicate floral design of rich burgundy and black. An ornate wooden railing steadied her as she navigated up the winding path.

More dim lighting greeted her at the top level, candles flickering through etched brass holders that cast lovely designs on the shadowy walls. Velvet curtains stood in various positions of opened and closed, with private supper booths behind each, or rather—as it seemed to Caron—private compartments, almost as one might expect inside a train.

She wasn't led to one of these booths, but down another hall to several doors, each a different color and each displaying a sign: Red Room, Blue Room, Green Room. The gentleman attending Caron indicated a door.

"You will be dining in the Red Room this evening," he stated, turning the brass doorknob and motioning her inside.

Caron walked in front of him, a tiny hallway before her, the walls flickering with more candle-induced shadows. The air was laced with the soft scent of jasmine, a sensual tune floating through ceiling speakers. Behind her, the sound of the door gently closing sent a wave of anticipation climbing up Caron's spine.

Suddenly, strong arms wrapped around her from behind, proving Baxter had followed her into the hallway without her knowing.

"You're late," he purred in a whiskey-smooth voice near her ear.

"I wasn't sure I was coming," she said, her voice shuddering with the feeling of his legs and hips settling against hers, molding her close.

"Then why did you?"

Her mind raced with the proper way to answer. "I have to send the wig back tomorrow. You're leaving tomorrow. It was now or never."

He chuckled, low and inviting, and turned her in his arms. His tie was gone, his shirt unbuttoned—a tiny sprinkling of dark hair peeked through the top. "So it's all about the wig, is it?"

"Isn't it?" she challenged, holding her breath as she waited for his answer.

"The wig was for the press," he promised, tugging at the pins and tossing them aside. The wig came next. "You're for me."

Caron barely kept herself from holding the wig in place, as he removed it. She used her fingers to shake her natural hair free.

"You have no idea how badly I wanted to do that in the store today." He took her hand. "Come. Drink some wine with me."

He led her toward the table and Caron willed her heart to stop racing. Because whatever happened tonight, there was no bombshell image to hide behind.

# 9

WHAT CARON DID TO HIM, well, it had him in knots, had him burning with the need to do so much more than simply shove her skirt to her waist and bury himself inside her body—though that sounded damn good right now.

Relentless desire tightened his groin as Baxter held Caron's chair out, his gaze flickering across the subtle glimpse of thigh as she settled into the seat. The hard thrum of lust pumped through his veins, his mind filled with illicit fantasies the private room allowed. In the back of his mind, he told himself to act on those things, take Caron now, forget dinner. After all, this was about sex—about a fantasy. And sex was sex, plain and simple. A way to relieve a little tension, fulfill that deep primal need all men accepted as a part of living, and then refocus on the performance pressure of running Remington—the pressure to come through for family, for stockholders, for his employees. Or at least that's how it had always been in the past. Until Caron. Suddenly, plain and simple wasn't so simple.

Clamping down on his male urges, Baxter managed a facade of nonchalance as he claimed the seat across from Caron and studied her, trying to connect with what it was about her that had him practically shaking with desire. And normally he didn't shake. Not for a woman. Not in business. He had to know why he did for her.

She blinked at him, then her lashes fluttered closed, dark half circles on pale skin, relaying that quality of genuine vulnerability he'd found himself drawn to. Vulnerability that contrasted with the inner strength and confidence she also managed quite magnificently. Qualities that said she wouldn't let fear defeat her—that she could, and would, survive whatever life threw at her.

Eager to draw her into conversation, to learn more about her, Baxter opened a menu. "Everything is excellent. Steaks, fish, pasta."

"Allergic to fish," she said. "So better pass on that. I, ah, swell up kind of like a blowfish." He laughed and she flushed. "Too much information," she quickly added. "Really don't want you picturing that right about now. But anyway, ah, never loved the taste or the smell of seafood anyway, so it's no real loss." She crinkled her nose. "The smell especially."

He chuckled at her adorable rambling, already quite familiar with that being her way of dealing with stress, nerves, anything spinning out of control. "Not fond of the taste or smell myself," he said, surprised at that parallel in their lives. "Not many people understand that, here in San Fran." He pointed to a section of the menu. "So on that note, let me recommend the chicken."

She grinned her appreciation. "Chicken sounds good."

They went on to debate several food choices before

both deciding on two orders of chicken Marsala, which he could personally recommend. Once decided, Baxter hit the buzzer on the table and ordered their meal.

Caron scanned the elegantly decorated Red Room. "Private themed rooms. Ordering over an intercom." Her eyes widened. "I've never seen anything like this place."

"They cater to a crowd that prefers discretion in both business and pleasure," he said, filling her glass with wine. "They do it well."

Caron picked up her glass and inhaled. "Smells wonderful."

"It's Jordan cabernet from a local vineyard," he supplied. "One of my favorites."

She sipped, her lips stained the same red from Friday night. He stared at that lovely mouth, his groin tightening as he thought of kissing her. Of tasting her sweetness one more time.

"It's wonderful," she murmured. "I do love a good red wine." She set her glass down. "My grandmother retired from the state library this past year and moved to the Sonoma area. It's a great excuse to do some local wine sampling but with the demands of the store, I'm always rushing there for a visit and then rushing right back."

"I guess her career explains your love for books as easily as my father's explains mine for coffee," he commented.

"Oh, yes. My mother was a librarian. It's in the blood, I think. I guess that goes for you, as well, considering you run the family business."

"It does for me but not my three sisters. They want

nothing to do with coffee. Two of them are teachers like my mother. The youngest is in law school at the University of Texas in Austin."

"So it's been all you, then, running the show."

"Oh, no," he said. "I'd do a disservice to my father to claim any of this success was about me. I simply learned from the best and grabbed the reins when he retired. This was his dream and his hard work. He opened the first store right here in the city before I was even born. The only store until I was almost ten."

"Really?" she said. "There must be hundreds of locations now."

"Thousands," he amended, unable to stop the pride simmering in his voice. "But it was a struggle, and a lot of years, to get here. He used what little savings we had and commuted from Oakland daily and still had moments when he was certain he'd failed."

Surprise flickered across her face. "And here I thought you were born with a silver spoon in your mouth," she teased.

He snorted at that, thinking of the harder times in his youth. "Plastic is more like it," he amended. "And we washed those for multiple uses for a lot of years. My father struggled to compete against bigger name brands."

"That's how I feel about the big bookstores," she said, her elbows settling on the table, her chin on her hands, genuine interest in her expression. "So what turned it around?"

"He finally broke down and brought in a private investor, which meant letting go of some stock but it also gave him the cash to compete. A year later he was managing stores in several malls and another inside

Turnball's department store. From there, things sky-rocketed."

"And coffee lovers around the world rejoiced," she chimed in, applauding softly before resting her hands on the edge of the table as if hiring herself back to reality. "One successful store will be enough for me, though, I believe."

He'd seen her in that store today, the special touches so clearly her own, and he believed her. Ruling the world was not on her agenda. Nor was using him to do it. "And what would make your store a success in your mind?" he asked, exceedingly interested in her goals and dreams.

"Paying my grandmother back the money she loaned me to open the store, for starters." Her answer was quick, certain. "That's huge to me. She not only raised me, but she's always believed in me. I want her to know it was for a good reason." She ran her fingers down the etched stem of her glass. "Funny thing—or not so funny really—I don't remember much about my mother, but she loved books. She and my grandmother dreamed of opening a bookstore together. Now, my grandmother says she's living vicariously through me."

She only had her grandmother. He wondered if that wasn't part of that vulnerability he sensed in her. "Why vicariously?"

Her eyes sparkled and she leaned forward as if sharing a secret. "She seems to have another interest now. I think the retired fireman who pops into the library she's volunteering at might have a thing or two to do with it. I can hardly believe how smitten she is." Caron eased back into her chair again. "My grandma!

Unbelievable. I mean Grandpa passed a good thirty years ago, and this is the first time I've ever seen her take to another man. It's actually pretty fun to watch."

"My parents have been married forty-five years," he said with pride, but his mind was on a burning question he couldn't hold back. "Can I ask what happened to your parents?"

Solemnly, but without hesitation, she answered. "I lost them a long time ago—when I was five. My father was an architect who'd been invited to bid on a project in China. It was a rare, unique opportunity, and he took my mother along for the preliminary evaluation. I, of course, being so young, stayed home with my grandmother." A bit wearily, she inhaled and then exhaled. "While they were there, they chartered a plane from one location to another and, well, that was how it ended."

His gut twisted with that news. Five and no parents. "It must have been hard growing up without them," he commented, prodding gently for more insight into this woman who drew his interest more with each passing word.

Staring at the wineglass, her eyes turned down, she stroked the stem a bit more. His gaze caught on her long, delicate fingers. Everything about her intrigued him. "I think maybe it's easier at that age than being older and losing your parents. There is an emptiness inside me, yes, but not the kind of pain that comes with vividly remembering someone you've loved and lost. It's more indefinable." She let out a brittle, humorless laugh. "But then, as sure as I say that, I feel guilty for the absence of emotion—they are the people who brought me into this world." Emotion laced her next confession, "Sometimes that freaks me out a little. Not being able to clearly recall their faces. It sends me rushing to the photo album, trying to picture them in my mind again." She studied him carefully. "Again, probably way more than you wanted to know." She swirled her wine gently. "I blame the wine for making my tongue waggle."

"Then I'm glad for the wine," he said, lifting his glass in a mock salute, a moment before their eyes locked and held. The room seemed to heat, shared intimacy wrapping around them just as a blanket might. Then, he gently, seductively teased, "I find myself wanting to understand more about you than your inability to properly define the word nice." His pulse pounded in his temples, desire rocketing through his body. He leaned back in his chair before he caved to his desire, reached around the table and pulled her onto his lap.

More and more, he knew he wasn't going to be fair to her. She created a burn in him, a burn that wasn't going to be sated anytime soon. All he would do is drag her into the mess he was going through. She was just so damn *real*. He needed that right now. Needed it in a way that made it hard to do what was right. Which was walk away. Maybe he could make her do it for him. "You should run from me right now, Caron. Get far away from me before I've got you into something you don't want to be part of."

She tilted her head to one side. "Because of the accusations made against your VP?"

His lips thinned. "You've seen the papers, I presume?"

"Not before Friday night," she assured him. "But since then…yes…I was curious enough to look you up."

Again, her honesty. No coyness. No games. "Then you know why I worried about that dance Friday night. Why I've tried to keep you from the press."

"It must be difficult," she said, not directly commenting on his statement. "Trying to seem impervious to onlookers, even those close to you who trust you to make it all turn out okay."

"The hardest damn thing I've ever done in my life," he found himself admitting, despite the warning in his head telling him to stay silent. But the truth was, he had no one to talk to but Caron. Everyone else did expect him to be the steel behind the crisis. "My father is taking the entire thing far more smoothly than I am, but then he's in Europe on vacation—rather removed from it all. And Jett is someone I've considered a friend. That makes this more difficult to swallow."

"Jett," she said. "That's the VP accused of securities fraud."

He gave a quick nod. "I would have sworn he was innocent."

"Would have?"

"His absence is pretty damning," he said, repeating what he'd only said in his head until this point. "Why run if you're innocent?"

She dismissed that immediately. "Fear and stupidity don't equal guilt. And fear makes people do stupid things."

He paused to consider her and then laughed. "You just say whatever you think, don't you?"

"Every time I've ever tried not to, it's backfired. If my foot is going to end up in my mouth, I, at least, want to be speaking the truth when it lands there."

"I guess that makes sense," Baxter said, smiling yet again as he sipped his wine.

Caron did the same and then said, "It sure beats that bitter champagne from the party Friday." She sniffed. "Though I very uncharacteristically did it more justice than it deserved."

"And why was that?"

"Are you kidding me?" she asked, giving him a disbelieving look. "It was hard enough to walk down that runway with all those people watching. But I wasn't exactly expecting to be Marilyn Monroe that night." She sipped her wine. "And I can blame my plumbing for that one. I was late and they gave my Audrey costume away, which was why I told you to look for Audrey when we met. Then the woman scheduled to be Marilyn broke her ankle, and next thing I knew— poof. I was blonde and wearing a dress with cleavage to the waist. I was terrified."

"Speaking from close observation," he said, "you owned the runway and the costume. You certainly got my attention."

"I thought it was the sweat suit," she countered.

"Oh, it was," he assured her. "That and the way you told the doorman about your plumbing problems."

She grimaced. "He didn't seem to understand my urgent parking situation."

The buzzer on the table went off, and Baxter hit a button. The door to the room opened, and their food was served.

As they began their meal, to his surprise, he found himself thoroughly engaged in conversation, forgetting all the reasons to keep Caron at a distance. Debates arose over politics, the state of the city council, and even who made the better James Bond. He couldn't remember a dinner that he had enjoyed more in recent times, if ever. And for the second time in two weeks, both occasions in Caron's company, Baxter found himself relaxing.

A good hour after dinner was served, Baxter and Caron relocated to a sitting room attached to the dining area where they sat on a plush red couch that faced huge double-paned windows overlooking the ocean. Slices of chocolate cake and cups of coffee sat untouched on the rectangular table before them, the magnetic pull of their attraction darn near combustible.

He turned to her, their knees touching. "I did bring you here to prove a point, you know?"

She smiled. "I know."

"Are you going to give me that opportunity?"

"I'm still deciding," she said. "Perhaps you should give me a reason."

"Friday night was—"

"Memorable," she provided, the glint in her eyes saying she knew he wouldn't like that description any more than the *nice* orgasm.

His hand slid around her neck, his mouth lowering to linger above hers; a soft floral scent flared in his nostrils. A silky strand of hair fell gently to his cheek. "You enjoy teasing me, don't you?"

"I believe I do," she replied, leaning into him, fingers pressing into his chest, promising sultry caresses to follow.

He laughed, so damn taken with her frankness, with the sweetness that was so purely Caron. "Do you know that a Red Door is symbolic of passion to many—to others, a sanctuary?" He didn't intend for her to answer, didn't give her a chance. "That's why I chose the Red Room. So it could be our little sanctuary." His lips feathered over hers. "I'm going to make love to you, Caron," he whispered. "And there isn't going to be anything *nice* about it."

"Promises, promises," she whispered just before he slanted his mouth over hers, his tongue pressing past her teeth with a hungry kiss that answered her teasing with more than a promise—it answered with proof.

## 10

IT WAS OFFICIAL. Caron had become a wanton vixen, and she should immediately cease to act so brazenly. And she would. Right after she kissed Baxter just a little bit longer. Just a kiss—a nice, deep, sensual kiss. With lots of serious tongue. No one would know. There was that red door protecting her from exposure. Oh, yes. She liked that red door. And she liked Baxter. So much. Too much.

And just as she'd hoped, long, deep strokes of Baxter's tongue delivered the promised kiss, working her over, reason slipping further from the forefront of her mind. His hand slid up her thigh, under her dress, and Caron felt her legs inch apart, boldly encouraging him to move higher. She didn't know what had happened to her since she donned that blond wig, or maybe she did—Baxter had happened. He had swept into her life and taken her on a roller-coaster ride of passion sure to end with her being heartbroken. But somehow she couldn't seem to care. Nor did she think twice when his lips, and then his hands, lured her to his lap, her legs spread wide, dress hiked to her waist as she straddled him. He was hard, his erection straining against the zipper of his slacks, the thin material doing nothing to disguise the thick ridge of his impressive bulge. That didn't help her muster any willpower, considering she knew just how impressive his cock was. She pressed against him, fought the urge to rock, but found it nearly impossible. She was losing her mind with need, losing herself to desire.

Suddenly, the buzzer on the door sounded with warning. Caron tore her lips from Baxter's. "Oh, God." She tried to escape his lap. But his hands settled on her waist, held her in place.

"They won't come in unless I hit the remote entry button."

Her eyes were wide, her heart fluttering wildly in her chest. "What? Where?"

"On the same remote I ordered dinner from."

"You're sure?"

"Positive," he assured her, his hands gliding up and down her sides to create a soothing sensation. Slowly, she eased into him, allowed him to lure her lips to his.

And then the buzzer went off again. A voice sounded through the mike on the remote control. "There's an urgent call for you, Mr. Remington."

Baxter sighed in defeat and pressed his forehead to hers. "I'm sorry."

Something in his voice reached out to her, told of something more than regret. She leaned back, searched his chiseled features, his furrowed brow. Exhaustion haunted the depths of his eyes, the kind born of far too much stress.

Her fingers curved his jaw. "It's okay." She grabbed the remote from the coffee table and handed it to him. "Talk to whoever you have to talk to and get it over with." She offered a soft smile. "Then we can eat that chocolate cake."

He brought her fingers to his lips and smiled in return, but it didn't quite reach his eyes. "That sounds perfect." Caron slid off his lap; she quickly tugged her clothing back into place as he hit the speaker on the remote and said, "What line?"

"The caller said he would ring again in exactly ten minutes," came the response. "That was three minutes ago, sir. I'll put him through to your room when he calls if that meets your satisfaction?"

"It does," Baxter said, his brows furrowing all over again.

Caron gave him a keen inspection. "What's troubling you?"

He scrubbed his jaw, then rested his elbows on his knees. "Anyone who I'd want to talk to would call my cell phone."

Caron tucked her hair behind her ears and made the obvious assumption. "Reporters?"

"Or the damn FBI," he grumbled. "No matter how many times I tell them I don't know where Jett is, they insist I do."

Caron swallowed her guilt. She should tell him about being approached. She would tell him. However, this moment didn't seem exactly right.

The phone mounted on the far left wall near the window rang. Baxter pushed to his feet, and Caron stood, as well, thinking he might want privacy. "I'll go to the ladies' room," she told him.

He gave her a quick, appreciative nod—she had no doubt he was embarrassed by all of this. By the time she reached the door, Caron heard him answer the line, and then the muffled, "Where the hell have you been?"

*Jett,* she thought. Caron's stomach churned with this knowledge, with the fact that she might know something she didn't want to know. She wasn't certain, and she didn't want to be. The truth was, she liked Baxter, probably far more than she should. Maybe she wasn't fully objective anymore. The less she knew, the better.

Exiting to the hallway, Caron found it empty, flickering with those candles that could be sexy or spooky, depending on the moment, and right now, spooky seemed more like it. Where the heck was everyone? All behind closed doors, she thought, and doing naughty things, like the things she and Baxter were about to do.

Oh, wow! She stopped dead in her tracks. Was Dinner Club a translation for Sex Club? Suddenly, Caron felt nauseous.

Quickly she rushed toward the double-pillar archway that seemed a logical restroom entrance. Up ahead, a woman in a conservative business suit walked through the pillars, a briefcase and purse in hand. Male voices sounded, and Caron paused as the woman greeted three men, their legal chatter beginning almost instantly. Attorneys here on business, she surmised quickly.

Caron let out a relieved breath. This was not a sex club. Good grief, that Agent Walker and then that phone call had her paranoid. Of course Baxter had not brought her to a sex club!

Marginally less tense, Caron found the ladies' room and entered the marble-tiled sitting room finished in blues and grays that adjoined several restroom stalls.

Caron claimed the edge of a soft love seat and let her face fall into her hands. How did she end up in this ritzy place, with a rich, sought-after guy, who incidentally happened to be involved in a nasty legal scandal? She should run away, as he said. Do so quickly and decisively—leave—do not pass go, do not collect two hundred dollars, which in this case translated to, do not collect another orgasm.

"Seems you weren't completely honest with me, Ms. Avery."

Caron jumped at the unexpected female voice, her hands going to the edge of the seat. To her utter dismay, as if conjured up by her thoughts, Agent Walker stood before her. And she was looking far more intimidating in a black pantsuit, her hair twisted in a knot at the back of her head, than she had in her blouse and jeans in their previous encounter.

Caron's mouth went dry, her throat tight. "I thought this was a private club."

Agent Walker shoved her jacket aside to indicate the badge hooked to her belt. "I've got the ultimate entry pass," she boasted and then added drily, "Bet you wish I didn't, right about now." She crossed her arms in front of her ample bosom and tapped a high-heeled foot. "Don't play me for a fool," she said. "You weren't going to see Baxter Remington again, but yet here you are."

A defensive, rushed response flew from her lips. "I didn't plan to. I didn't. He came—" She bit back the rest of the words. This was not the FBI's business. She owed them no explanation of her personal life. She might not be a pushy witch like this woman, but her grandmother had not raised a *pushover,* either. "I've done nothing wrong. Going to dinner with this man does not make me a felon nor does anything I've heard from you, or the media, indicate he's a criminal. This is harassment."

Agent Walker cast her a dubious stare and then sat down on the love seat. She sighed, ran her hands down her legs. "Okay. I'm forgetting my badge for a minute and talking woman to woman. Baxter Remington is hot. I get that. He's rich. I get that, too."

"I don't care about his money!" Caron objected, offended.

Agent Walker held her hands up stop-sign fashion. "Sorry. My point is simply that a man like Baxter can lead a girl to the wrong place. I know, believe me. I've had my Baxter, and I don't want to go for that ride ever again."

Caron pursed her lips. "He's not leading me anywhere."

"Good," she said with enough bite to the reply to seem as if she really meant it. "Don't let him. Many a good person has fallen for the wrong person and regretted the outcome. Don't let that be you. Remember this—if you find out Baxter is involved in any illegal activity, or even that he knows where his VP is…and you don't say something…then you've crossed a line of guilt yourself." She fixed Caron in a steady stare. "Don't cross that line. Come to me. Let me help." She handed Caron a card, pressed it into her hand. "Call me any time of the day or night. I'm not the enemy. I'm a friend."

Without another word, Agent Walker pushed to her feet, her high heels clicking a taunting rhythm on the tiled floor as she departed.

Caron sat there, nails digging into the velvet cloth of the seat, and willed herself to think logically, not to panic. She wasn't going to get in trouble because she'd done nothing wrong. Right now, the only thing she was a part of was a two-night stand. Baxter was going out of town, and most likely that would be the end of their little adventure. Which was good. Because that kept her out of this FBI trouble for one thing. And it kept her from doing something crazy, like falling for him.

Her gaze traveled to the expensive painting on the lounge wall. Right. He wasn't right for her anyway. The man lived in a world where the bathroom decorations cost more than the plumbing bill she couldn't afford to pay. So what if he was funny, charming, and kissed like Don Juan—or the way she assumed Don Juan must have kissed.

Caron pushed off the seat and once again found herself straightening her clothes but with the full intention of seeing them messed up again. She had been Baxter's Marilyn; he'd just have to be her Don Juan tonight. And then she'd end their short acquaintance with a delicious memory-worthy kiss before saying goodbye.

"I'M NOT GOING TO JAIL for something I didn't do," Jett hissed through the phone line at Baxter. "The Feds manufactured their so-called proof. They want me to go down."

That accusation didn't sit well with Baxter. He'd believed Jett innocent but doubts were forming. "And why would they want that?"

"You tell me," he growled. "The corrupt bastards are obviously covering something up."

Baxter clamped down on the budding anger threatening to surface. "Your attorney will deal with it. Running isn't the answer. Aside from shaking up your family and friends, it's made Remington's stockholders uneasy." His lips thinned. "And that is putting employees' jobs on the line."

"Fuck the stockholders! I *am not* going to jail."

"Then why are you calling?" he said. "What do you want from me?"

"I can't get to my funds right now," he said. "I need help. I need money."

Money. He wanted money? Not a chance in hell. Baxter ground his teeth and issued an undeserved warning. "If you haven't turned yourself in by Monday, I'm going to the FBI myself."

"You don't know anything to tell the FBI," he blasted back. "What happened to friendship, Remington? Or is that reserved for only those lining your pockets at the time?"

"Friendship and my dire need to believe in you," Baxter replied in a steely voice, "are the only reasons I'm giving you until Monday."

"Don't hold your breath," he spout out. The line went dead.

"Damn it," Baxter cursed, his hand holding the receiver in a death grip. "Damn it."

He replaced the phone on the cradle. Ran a hand through his hair and stood, feet rooted into the carpet, pulse pounding in a fierce beat, his temple throbbing.

Baxter was loyal to those he trusted, loyal to those who counted on him. But he expected the same loyalty in return. He'd given that loyalty to Jett. A decision that was fast appearing to be a bad one, a decision that had hurt other people—his family, his employees, those people who'd believed their company a worthy investment. And he had no one to blame but himself. He'd hired Jett, vetted him through a process that had left only himself as the final decision-maker. Trusted Jett to make decisions in the best interest of the company, and its stakeholders, not his own interests.

Tension balled in his muscles and he started pacing. It felt like the world was caving in on him. Night after night, day after day, he had bled for this company, worked tirelessly to build success—so many times with Jett by his side. Had it all been a lie? A setup for ultimate betrayal? Or had Jett simply found trouble and not known how to get out of it? Not that it really mattered either way—Jett had chosen the wrong path regardless. And Baxter knew in his core that Jett wasn't going to turn himself in. Baxter would be forced to turn on Jett.

A knock sounded and his head jerked toward the door. Caron. He'd forgotten to give her the remote. He inhaled the soft scent of her perfume, still lingering on his skin. The sweet taste of her lips still flavoring his tongue. Meeting her had been the only escape he'd found from all of this; she was the only person who'd made him smile, made him forget. And he needed to forget now. He needed to get lost in Caron. He hit the remote, a primal, wild burn pulsing through his veins as he charged toward the door.

CARON BARELY CROSSED the threshold of the Red Room before she found herself wrapped in Baxter's embrace and drawn into a long, drugging kiss. One of his hands laced roughly through her hair, the other wrapped around her hips and then curved along her backside. It was a hungry, desperate kiss laden with emotion. He pressed her against the wall, tugged her leg to his waist. Pressed the long, hard length of his erection between her thighs. Caron moaned with the intimacy of it.

His lips brushed her ear. "I want you, Caron," he murmured hotly, one hand cupping her breast, unmercifully caressing her nipple.

Another moan escaped her lips, but she sensed the wildness in him, the shift in emotion to something dark and out of control. This was not the man she'd left minutes before.

"Baxter," she gasped. Her hands pressed into his shoulders, her chin tilted upward as she searched his face. She noted the tortured look in his eyes for a flash before he kissed her again, his tongue relentlessly demanding.

Caron fought the meltdown overtaking her, the fast tumble into passion quickly destroying her will to resist. She stopped kissing him. "Baxter! Wait. Please. Are you okay? You seem—"

"I will be once I'm inside you," he murmured hoarsely, reaching between her legs and sliding a finger beneath her panties to stroke her sensitive flesh. "Ah, so wet."

She gasped with the intimate invasion, panting as he slid a long finger inside her. Yes, she was wet. Embarrassingly so, considering she'd barely walked in the door, and they were both still fully clothed.

"Baxt—" A hot, primal kiss swallowed her intention to object, though she wasn't quite sure why she felt the need to do so. Except there was something different about him, something wild, unleashed—dark. But she had no will to fight, no will to debate the difference in one pleasure over the other. Caron whimpered helplessly into the possessive kiss, the invasion hot, demanding—the licks, nips and strokes taking her to the shadows of all-consuming passion.

She barely knew when he picked her up, scooped up her backside with his hands and carried her to the couch. Willingly she straddled him, her skirt hiked to her upper thighs as his heavy-lidded stare dropped to the red silk panties she wore, his thick lashes lowered. His fingers formed a V around her clit, the wet silk of her panties shoved aside as he teased the sensitive nub.

His gaze lifted to hers, held her spellbound, touched her in a way that his hands, and even his mouth, could not. It made her shiver from the inside out with the depth of passion radiating between them. A second later, it was as if their connection snapped. Moving as one, their mouths slanted together in a crazy, hot kiss, hands desperately traveling each other's bodies.

Baxter's pants were soon unzipped, his thick erection shoving aside her panties, the steely hard length sliding along the slick, swollen lips of her core. Caron writhed against him, burning to feel him inside her. That was all she could think. Get. Him. Inside her.

And so she made it happen, slipping his silky head past her sensitive lips, and pulling him into the depths of her body.

"Condom," he half whispered, half moaned, and she took him deeper.

"Pill," she panted and then had a moment of clarity that drew embarrassment. Her hands went to his shoulders. Her eyes latched on to his. "I'm not on it to have sex. I mean—it's not because I do this all the time." She didn't want him thinking she had some disease. "I don't. It's because—" He covered her mouth with his, and she never finished the explanation.

Wild kisses and long, hard strokes of his cock followed. Their bodies melded, hips rocked. Wild. So wild. Caron had never felt so hot and out of control. They moaned into a fast, hard rhythm that had her pumping her hips, had him thrusting his. Had her leaning back to find that perfect spot that delivered a new surge of energy. That spot that said release was in sight, that it was one more swivel of her hips…just one more. Or maybe one more. That feeling that drove her to keep going, to keep reaching.

"Oh, yeah, baby," Baxter moaned, and her body spasmed around the hard length of him, buried oh-so-deliciously deep inside her—pulling at him, taking and taking.

He thrust again and again, then exploded inside her, hips lifting her, hands pressing her hard against him. Caron buried her face in his neck, clung to him as their bodies climbed to release. Her body melted against that rock-hard chest, melted into those powerful arms as they closed around her.

For a long while afterward, they lay there as one, unmoving, satisfied, a wonderfully comfortable silence between them. His hand stroked through her hair.

Reality slowly seeped into Caron's mind, and she sensed a heaviness in Baxter's emotions. Seeking confirmation, she shifted, searching his face. One look into his turbulent eyes, and she whispered, "Are you okay?"

"It was Jett." A stark quality touched his low voice. "On the phone."

Her stomach knotted. There was the information she didn't want to know. Didn't need to know. But now she did. Now there was no place to go but into the fire. "And?"

A muscle in his jaw jumped. "I gave him until Monday to turn himself in or I'll go to the authorities."

Relief washed over her. He was the man she'd sensed. A man of honor who would do the right thing. "What did he say?"

He grimaced. "In short. That I'm a self-serving bastard." The betrayal he felt etched his face.

She touched his cheek. "You're doing the right thing. Don't let him get to you."

He drew her hand into his, examined her expression. "You should stay away from me." The words were spoken as if he felt he had to say them. As if he didn't want to say them.

"I know," she whispered, wishing it weren't true, knowing it was.

"I could drag you into something you don't want any part of. Probably already have."

She nodded. "I know that, too."

His hand caressed her waist. "I want you to come home with me, Caron. Tell me, no."

"No," she murmured, their eyes locking, the magnetic pull of their attraction crackling in the air because they both knew no meant yes. And that Caron was already in the fire, already burning with the heat of a bad position that felt too good to deny. At least tonight. Tomorrow, she told herself, was a new day. Tomorrow she'd say no and mean no.

But not today.

# *11*

AFTER A DECADENT NIGHT of lovemaking, conversation, and more lovemaking, morning arrived far too early—especially considering Caron had to be at work, and Baxter had to catch a flight to Texas. Just before 8 a.m., wearing only Baxter's T-shirt, Caron fumbled her way around his barren kitchen cabinets and managed to find two mugs. She filled them with the piping hot coffee she'd brewed and then mixed in some vanilla creamer before heading back to the bathroom where she'd left Baxter to shave. It seemed coffee supplies were the only plentiful thing in Baxter's kitchen.

"Coffee is served," she said, finding Baxter at the bathroom sink with shaving cream slathered over his jaw, looking sexier-than-sin in nothing but boxers. Blue. With little black checks on them. Her gaze traveled his long, muscular legs brushed with dark hair. She really liked his legs. But then, she liked a lot about Baxter.

She set the cup next to him on the marble counter-top and then claimed a seat on the tiled step leading to the gorgeous sunken tub, tucking the T-shirt under her backside. "A few hours from now, you are going to hate me for keeping you up all night," she said, her palms wrapped around the mug, the warmth heating her chilly hands. "What time did you say your flight is?"

"Eleven o'clock." He stopped shaving long enough to cast her a look in the mirror. "And you were well worth some lost sleep."

Her eyes met his and the spark of that connection sent a warm flush over her skin. "We'll see if you say that a few hours from now," she teased.

"I'll be fine," he insisted, refocusing on the task of shaving. "I'll sleep on the plane."

For several seconds, Caron was spellbound by the way he moved, the way he held the razor. She'd never known a man so powerfully male—so dominantly present in every room he entered—yet, still so gentle and unassuming in all the right ways.

"I've never liked sleeping on planes," she said finally, trying to snap herself out of this lusty longing for more Baxter, when the goodbyes were about to come. The final goodbyes. "I always worry about doing something silly in my sleep like snoring. Not that I snore, but what if I chose a public place to start? Or what if I drool?" She shuddered.

He cast her an amused glance and chuckled. "You've given this some thought, I see."

"I flew to one of my suppliers' distribution centers a few months back and did so with very little sleep. My eyes kept trying to shut on the plane but, needless to say, I managed to stay awake." She sipped her coffee. "Hmm," she said. "Remington coffee is pretty darn good."

"But expensive," he said, reminding her again of her verbal faux pas when they'd first met.

"Way, way expensive," she joked, glad to take his

bait. "You should have a day a week that is some sort of budget promotion for people like me."

He snagged the towel on the rack and wiped his face, turning to study her with a thoughtful expression on his face. "That's not a bad idea. Not bad at all." Absentmindedly, he ran light fingers over his cleanly shaven jaw, checking his work. "I've been looking for ways to bring positive attention instead of negative, and get my stockholders excited again. This might fit into that agenda." He homed in on her. "That is, if you don't mind me stealing your idea?"

"I'd be thrilled if you used it." Her mind started to race, and she set her cup on the edge of the tub and straightened. "You could do it in a way that generates revenue for you, too, which logically would please stockholders. Pick the time of day you sell the least coffee and offer incentives during those times. It's affordable for people with less money and you generate revenue you wouldn't normally generate without cutting into your expected sales. Maybe some sort of catchy saying that you use to promote it—'The Remington two-dollar, two-hour dash.'" She cringed. "Okay. Forget I said that. Something better, but snappy."

He reached for her and pulled her to her feet, lifting her and setting her on the sink, slicking a strand of her hair behind one ear. "It's adorable, just like you."

Adorable. She had never liked *adorable. Cute* was even worse. Her stomach started to roll. Who was she fooling? Baxter wanted a bombshell. Why else had he sent her that package? "I guess I have to put the wig back on to be sexy?"

His finger slid under her chin, his eyes held hers. "You're adorable *and* sexy," he said, his voice a bit smoky, a bit aroused. She liked aroused and liked when he added, "It's a perfect combination."

She wanted to believe he meant that, but she was afraid to. "So suave," she rebutted, her fingers threading through the soft dark hair of his chest, despite the ache in her heart. "You must be very good with the ladies."

"Just one, I hope," he promised, and slid a hand around her neck, fingers tickling her with sensation as they caressed, but he offered no more reassurances. Both his expression and his tone sobered as he said, "I'm worried about you getting out of here unnoticed. The press has been stalking me. When I leave, I'll make sure I'm seen so they think hanging around here is unnecessary. But your safest exit is to wait awhile, stay here and get some rest if you want. I can have a car on standby for you in the basement, and you should be able to slip out unnoticed."

Surprised, she asked, "You want me to stay in your apartment when you leave?" She wasn't sure she understood correctly. Surely not.

"That's right," he told her. "Make yourself at home. Sleep. Take a bath. Explore the library upstairs and make sure I meet your book quota for a home." His lips lifted with that last suggestion. "Whatever pleases you. I'd feel better if you waited awhile to leave."

"But I have to open the store."

"I know this is an imposition, and I feel like a selfish bastard for bringing you here." He slid his hands to her face. "But I can't say I'm sorry because it would be a lie. Worried about you—yes. Sorry you came—no.

Kasey seemed like a nice, responsible girl. Can't she open for you?"

He was probably right, but she felt awkward staying here when he was gone. "Aren't you worried I'll snoop around? And what about locking up?"

"You have my permission to snoop," he said, amusement dancing in his eyes. "And I'll give you a key to lock up. I trust you to get it back to me. After all, you owe me a birthday gift for my sister, who incidentally is the ultimate snooper and does not have a key, so be sure to keep the key separate from the gift. If she gets her hands on it, she'd rearrange everything I own, and fill my kitchen with groceries that will go bad and that I'll end up throwing out. She thinks I live on coffee and takeout."

Caron laughed at that. He talked about his family a lot. She wondered if he knew how much. "Do you?"

"Yes, but I'd never admit that to her, and certainly not to my mother. Say yes to staying, Caron." His hands settled on her waist. "I need to know I didn't turn your life upside down."

Smooth like whiskey, his voice was a gentle caress, coaxing her into easy submission. "Okay," she whispered. "I'll stay." She could always leave once he'd gone.

A smile touched those sensual lips before he kissed her, a kiss that led to one last wonderful round of pleasure. A kiss that almost made her feel she really was his bombshell. At least for a little while longer.

An hour later, her body sated, her stomach knotted, Caron stood in the foyer of the apartment, with Baxter by the door preparing to depart. Dressed in a black pin-striped suit, he looked good enough to eat, a picture-perfect, hunky image to remember. Her chest tightened, fearful of the final, awkward goodbye she'd tried to avoid by leaving that first morning. But was it goodbye? Her mind kept going back to that key. Was it an excuse to see her again?

Contemplating that thought, she found herself wrapped in Baxter's arms, his spicy cologne teasing her nostrils. "I'll call you when I land and make sure you didn't have any trouble."

"You don't have to do that," she said, preferring that the end would just be the end. It was easier that way. "Really. It's not necessary."

"I know," he said, his hand lacing into her hair as he tugged her to him for a quick, but wonderful, kiss. And then he was gone; he'd turned away and walked out the door, leaving a trail of fine male-scented air in his wake. Leaving her to inhale that scent with bittersweet enjoyment, because he was gone, and all she had to look forward to was a bath in that big, wonderful tub—she wanted no part of sleep, no part of being in his bed without him in it with her.

THE PRIVATE CAR BAXTER had arranged dropped Caron at the back door of her apartment near eleven o'clock, and thankfully, she'd found no sign of reporters. She'd quickly changed clothes and rushed to the bookstore.

Caron parked her Volkswagen at the rear entrance of the store near lunchtime, and drew a deep breath, preparing to face the firing squad. Her bath had ended with a panicked call from Kasey; the store was swarming with more than customers. Apparently, several reporters were there, asking questions about Baxter. Seemed

Caron's escape from the limelight had been no escape at all. Someone other than the FBI had placed them together.

Dressed in a conservative blue pin-striped pantsuit and high-heeled boots, she shoved open the door of the car and started for the store. Another car door opened and shut, and a man in slacks and casual jacket was by her side.

"Ms. Avery," he said, shoving a picture at her which Caron refused to look at even though she wanted to— badly. "I'm Troy Wilkins with the *Times.* Can you tell me what your relationship with Baxter Remington is?"

Avoidance seemed as if it would invite more questions so she stopped. "I have no idea what you are talking about."

He shoved another picture at her. "Is this you?"

Caron glanced at the photo of her and Baxter dancing Friday night. "Yeah. So."

"And that's Baxter Remington. So what is your relationship with him?"

"The same as it was with every other guy I danced with that night. There is none. And I have no idea why you are asking this and why I am even answering. Please. I have to get to work."

"What do you say about this?" He flashed yet another picture at her. Of her the night before, leaving the dinner, but thankfully her face wasn't showing. Just the blond wig Baxter had insisted she put back on, along with a scarf the restaurant had managed to produce.

"The man has a thing for blondes," she said drily, a little punch in her gut at the truth behind those words…and the ones to follow. "As you can see," she continued, self-consciously touching the brunette knot tied at the back of her neck, "I don't fit that bill." She sidestepped the reporter and tried to close the short distance between where she stood and the door.

"You were blonde Friday night," he called after her. "Who says you weren't last night."

Caron's hand froze on the door, her teeth grinding. She whirled around and faced him. "Sounds like you need to write a story about your own kinky obsessions. I'm sure you've checked me out. I'm nothing but a good girl, through and through."

She gave him her back and yanked the door open but managed to hear his last snide remark, "The good girls are always the best at being bad."

Her heart sank at the realization that she'd failed to shut this guy down. In fact, if anything, she seemed to have given him an angle on a story. The press was on to her and no doubt, the FBI would be calling again, as well. Rattled, her mind raced with turbulent thoughts. What if Agent Walker asked about Jett? She didn't want to get in trouble, but she didn't want to get Baxter in trouble, either.

"Oh, Caron!" Kasey exclaimed, charging down the hall toward her, blond bob bouncing with her rushed pace. "What is going on with you and Baxter Remington?"

Caron quickly entered her office and sat down behind her desk, wishing for a rock to climb under.

Relentless in her demand for answers, Kasey stood directly in front of her. "And don't say nothing," she warned. "I already figured out he's that hot guy who was in here yesterday."

Caron dropped her purse into her desk drawer. "Don't you have customers to attend?"

Kasey shoved her hands onto her hips. "You aren't talking, are you?"

"Nope," Caron agreed. "So you might as well turn around and go back to work."

"Will you reconsider later?" she asked hopefully.

Caron glared. "Not a chance."

"Would it help erase that angry look on your face if I told you I called the police on the reporters?" she asked.

"Yes."

"I'll go do that right now," she said, and quickly turned away.

Relief washed through Caron at her departure and her intended actions. The store phone rang on the edge of her desk, and Caron could see one of the lights was lit, indicating Kasey had already dialed the police.

Accepting the inevitable, Caron feigned a cheerful greeting, and answered, "Book Nook, can I help you?"

Static crackled on the line. "You made it to work, I see," came the deep, sexy voice. Baxter. "Is everything okay?"

No, everything wasn't okay. Nothing was okay. More static. She avoided the loaded question. "Where are you?"

"Airport, between flights. Lots of bad weather and delays. I'm not getting good reception." More static. "Damn. It's bad here. Listen, sweetheart. I talked to our PR person about your idea. She loved it."

Sweetheart? "Really?" she asked, reasoning away the endearment as just casual guy talk and unable to be excited about his announcement. Any other time she would be. But the press, the FBI. She was trembling inside that she might say or do something wrong. "That's great, Baxter."

More static. "I can barely hear you, Caron. Give me your cell phone number, and I'll call you tonight when I get to a room."

She hesitated. Told herself not to. Found she had no willpower where he was concerned and rattled off her number. Twice, thanks to the static. Two times she had the chance to back down but she charged farther into the fire.

"It'll be late," he said. "Around ten."

"Have a safe flight," she said softly, emotions tightening her chest, but he was gone in a charge of static, the line disconnected.

Caron eased the phone back in the cradle and told herself she could not talk to him or see him again. What if the FBI came to her and asked about Jett? She knew he'd contacted Baxter. Caron could get Baxter in trouble. She could get herself in trouble. She had to stay away from him. But he was out of town, she reasoned. A call meant nothing.

So why was she worried. *A man like Baxter can lead a girl to the wrong place.* Agent Walker's words played in her head. Was Baxter leading her to a bad place? Had he already? Had all her will been destroyed because she was clearly falling for the man and falling hard. And even *he* had said, run away. Even he knew he was trouble.

She dropped her face into her hands. Taking his call tonight would not be smart, and she was a smart girl. Or she used to be. She wasn't sure anymore. Sadly, she realized she had no one to talk to. Her best friend had gotten married and moved to Europe the year before, and work had consumed Caron ever since. Her grandmother would go into protective mode. Kasey was too young, too naive. She'd tell Caron to jump back into bed and just enjoy. And why did she suddenly want to talk to Kasey?

"Caron," Kasey said, frowning in the doorway. "Did you call another plumber?"

"No," she replied, pushing to her feet. "I can't afford another plumber." She couldn't afford the last one.

"Well, there's a guy upstairs working on the toilet. Said he was instructed to fix it."

Caron rushed to the stairs, but not before noting the reporter from the parking lot in the store. She motioned to Kasey. "He's a reporter. Get him out of here."

"Okay, boss," she said. "And the police are on their way."

Standing in the doorway of the bathroom, Caron focused on the immediate issue of the plumber. "I didn't call you. I can't pay you," she blurted.

He glanced up at her. Flashed a badge that said Remington. "I'm on salary," he clarified. "I get paid no matter what. You need a new tank. I'll have you fixed up within the hour."

She couldn't believe Baxter was doing this. "I… How much is a tank?"

"My instructions were—this one's on the house."

Caron was blown away by this. Baxter was rich. She was poor. She wasn't overly sure how she felt about him taking care of this for her, although she couldn't deny that with her tight budget she was thankful.

Maybe it was nothing for him to flex some financial

muscle for a woman. For her, it was a big deal. A really big deal. She was raised to believe you made it on your own; you didn't let someone do things for you. And all her life she and her grandmother had managed. It was scary thinking of leaning on someone else. Not that one toilet made for dependency, but Caron was confused. Her plumbing problems were fixed, though. It seemed everything else grew more complex by the minute. Including her feelings for Baxter.

BAXTER SETTLED ONTO the delayed flight and leaned back in his seat, a smile touching his lips as he thought of Caron's reasoning for not sleeping on a plane. His lips twitched, a smile barely contained. Every bone in his body ached with tiredness, but Caron could still put a smile on his lips.

For the first time in his life, he couldn't get a woman off his mind, and that suited him fine. That was the crazy part. He liked this crazy feeling she provoked in him. He liked the way she made him laugh, the way she asked nothing but gave so much. Her way of thinking, her honesty. Her brains. God, he loved she had the brains and gumption to do her own thing. Her bookstore was unique; her idea for his stores, smart.

She didn't deserve to get drawn into this scandal of his, but he couldn't talk himself into walking away from her. It was stingy, selfish, and he knew it. Part of him hated himself for being so insensitive. But she was in his head. Hell, she was working her way to his heart if he was right about her. He couldn't not be with her. He just couldn't. Silently, he vowed to protect her, to take care of her and ensure none of this touched her life.

He frowned, thinking of Jett and his betrayal, thinking of how his father had always warned him to trust only family. He'd thought that was old-timer's thinking. Now, he wasn't so sure.

Already his attorney was plotting how Monday would go down, certain Jett wouldn't show. There would be negotiations, and most likely, Baxter would be used to lure Jett into custody. Baxter's gut twisted and he clung to the hope that Jett would prove his innocence. He still couldn't accept he had been this wrong about the man.

He closed his eyes and rested his head on the seat, thinking of something far more pleasurable—Caron. His mind replayed their lovemaking, her soft moans, and his cock hardened. There would definitely be no sleeping on this flight. Maybe none until he got back home to Caron.

# *12*

CARON LEANED AGAINST her cushioned headboard, snuggling under the white down comforter of her cushy quilt-top, queen-size bed, a bit before ten. Her cell phone rested on the white glossy nightstand nearby. She studied her tiny room, comparing it to the size of Baxter's master bathroom—thinking how different their worlds were. Sure, he came from nothing, but nothing for him was a long time ago. She lived in a world where her bed had been a rare splurge forced onto her when the springs of her old mattress had been popping out. The comforter was a gift from her grandmother. The books lining the shelves around her room, years of collecting. Her home wasn't fancy like Baxter's, but it was home—her home—and she didn't need the glitz of his world. But she did envy him the sense of security he must have—she longed for that and for the sense of achievement the store's long-term success would give her.

Beside her, the cell phone jangled and vibrated across the nightstand, and Caron knew without looking that it was Baxter. He was on time, dependable. Weren't playboys supposed to keep a girl hanging, make apologies for being late and then win forgiveness with fancy dinners and amazing orgasms?

That is what she expected from playboys, but then, Baxter had yet to be anything she'd expected and so much more than she'd hoped. Not that dinners and orgasms rested in their future, so perhaps Baxter saw no reason to play games with her. All the more reason to simply stop talking to him. To avoid trouble.

But the man had sent her a plumber. How could she not take his call? Not thank him? And it wasn't as though the plumber or this call meant anything. It was simply his way of dealing with his guilt about fears that his media frenzy might touch her—and it had.

The phone stopped ringing. She inhaled and sank down beneath the covers. Okay. Done. Decision made for her. No conversation. She'd send him a thank-you note for the plumber with his sister's present and his key. So why did disappointment settle hard in her stomach? She willed it away, but it dug deeper, bit harder.

The ringing began again. Caron jumped and sat back up. Nervously, she answered the phone, not about to ignore it a second time. "Hello," and to her distress found her voice cracked.

"Hello, Caron," he said, his voice low, smooth, intimate. "You didn't answer. I was afraid with all the static earlier that I heard the number wrong."

"No. You heard right."

"But you didn't answer."

"No."

"Why not?"

"I answered," she argued.

"You weren't going to talk to me," he accused.

Oh, well, heck. "Okay," she said. "Fine. Since you

clearly aren't going to let this go. You're right. I considered not talking to you."

"You didn't want to talk to me?"

"I did. I do. You confuse me, Baxter. We met one night. It was over. Then it was two nights. I'm never prepared for what comes next with you."

He laughed. "It's really good to hear your voice, Caron."

She had no idea what to say. Flirting had never been her thing, and she sort of thought they were flirting. Doing so over the phone was even less her thing. At least, seeing his face, she could read him better.

He seemed to read her hesitation and gave her a nudge, "This is where you are supposed to say—it is good to hear your voice, too, Baxter."

She could feel him smiling into the phone. "Oh," she said. "Of course. It is good to hear your voice, too, Baxter, and thank you for buying me a toilet."

"I bought you a toilet?" he asked, chuckling.

She loved that low rumbling chuckle. He did it often, and it always gave her a funny feeling in her stomach. "Yes," she said. "And it was quite the surprise. So was the plumber who showed up to install it."

"I've never bought a woman a toilet before. One of many firsts with you."

"That's good to hear because I have to tell you," she commented honestly, "if you went around buying women toilets, I'd be a little concerned. Though I do like mine."

He chuckled again, sending a shiver up her spine. "Not exactly the way to romance a girl. Next time, I'll make sure it's something far more romantic."

Next time? "You're trying to romance me?"

"What if I am?"

"Isn't it a little late for that?" she asked. "I mean—well, we kind of zoomed right past romance."

"Since when is making love all night long anything but romantic?" he disputed. "I'm sitting here in a downtown Austin hotel room, wishing I was there or you were here. I'm crazy about you, Caron."

She shook her head, rejected the heartache this was opening her up to. "You're crazy about the fantasy girl in a wig and gel bra. I'm not that girl, Baxter. I'm just a plain-Jane, hardworking girl whose bedroom is about the size of your shoe."

"Caron," he said softly, warmth reaching through the line and sliding along her skin. "There is nothing plain about you. Nothing. In fact, you are the most unique, dynamic person I think I've ever met. As for the fantasy—I found you in a pink sweat suit with no make-up on. That was the woman I wanted and still do."

Having a one- or two-night stand had been daring and out of character, but held limited risk. Falling for a guy like Baxter scared the heck out of her.

"I can't do this, Baxter," she said, thinking how easily he'd invaded her life, how easy it would be to get used to him being there. Then what happened when he was gone? "No. You're looking for an escape, and for whatever reason, you think I'm that. I'm not. And you aren't the one who'll get hurt. I will. I'm not up for that. I'm just not."

"I'm guilty as charged on at least one of your points, Caron, because you're right. I don't deny you're a welcome escape. You're genuine. What you see is what you get. I sat on that plane today and laughed as I thought about you talking about the possible mishaps of falling asleep while flying. You didn't even have to be with me to make me smile. Look, Caron. If you tell me to hang up the phone and never call again, so be it. But I don't want to. I want to stay on the line. I want to hear about your day. I want to hear about your life. Then, I want to come home to *you* and stay up all night long again, making love. Tell me you want that, too."

The emotions spoke to her more than the words. She was scared. Terrified. But she'd never let fear control her. "I do."

"Caron," he said softly. "You don't know how happy I am to hear that, and I swear to you," he said, "I'll do everything in my power to keep the press off your back."

"I know that." She spoke sincerely. "But we can kind of write that off as a done deal. They were waiting at my store today." She explained everything that had happened, including the police involvement. "They only have the wig shots, but it's just a matter of time before they are sure it's me."

"Come here with me," he offered. "Let me fly you out tomorrow morning where you can be close to me."

"I can't do that," she said. "I have a store to run. And I can't leave Kasey to deal with all of this. Besides. That would certainly tell them who I am."

"Sometimes coming out of hiding is best. After all, reporters love a good mystery to uncover. And I have to warn you. I have some tough choices to make between now and Monday that are most likely only going to make the press worse."

"Has he called again?" she asked, referring to Jett, but somehow feeling uncomfortable saying his name.

"No," he answered solemnly, clearly knowing who she referred to. How could he not? "And he's not going to. I've already accepted that this doesn't have a happy ending."

"I'm sorry." She felt the pain in his words, and wished she could help. The only way she knew how to do that was to listen. "Do you want to talk about it?"

"Yes," he said without hesitation. "Later. In person. Right now, I just want to talk period, to hear your voice. Tell me something good about your day."

She didn't want to tell him any more about the nightmare that her day was, so she bit back her inhibitions, and started with what came to mind, "Talking to *you* right now," she said. "Your voice is very soothing." And yet so damn arousing, but she didn't add that part. "Tell me about your new coffee shops. How many stores do you have there?"

For a good hour, he told her about his travels, about Texas. Fifteen minutes into the call, Caron flipped on her space heater and shoved the covers aside to rest on her stomach and elbows. Much to her surprise, she learned that the Remington "Two-Hour Dash" was being discussed as a fast-launch program.

She was flattered, but fretful. "What if it doesn't work, Baxter? I'm going to feel horrible that I suggested this if it bombs. I should never have said anything. I was just rambling."

"Nothing is going to go wrong. We try new things all the time. Some work, some don't. There is no failure in this, Caron. Only potential success. You worry too much."

"Me?" she scoffed. "Look who's talking."

"We aren't talking about me," he reminded her all too quickly. "We're talking about you."

"The ole double standard," she accused.

"Exactly," he agreed. "And I'm going to take on the management of your stress as my personal priority, starting right now. I'm going to take you through some relaxation techniques."

"Now?" she queried, frowning. "You're in Texas, in case you forgot."

"That is a bit of a problem," he agreed, mischief lifting in his voice. "I'm afraid I'll have to ask for your assistance. I'll make it up to you later."

"Okay," she replied, smiling. "I'll bite. I have no idea where you are going with this, but what assistance do you require?"

"I'm going to need you to pretend I am right there with you," he explained. "And I'll do the same. So first off, where are you?"

She was grinning now. "In bed."

"Me, too," he said. "But I hate hotel beds, so let's be in your bed instead of mine. Describe yours to me."

Her jaw dropped. "You want me to describe my bed."

"I'd rather see it for myself, but due to my limited navigational abilities at present, I'll settle for the description."

"Description," she repeated. "Okay. It's soft. Cushion top. Queen-size. Really soft, white down comforter. White sheets."

"Are you under the blanket?"

"No," she said. "Are you under yours?"

"I'm with you—remember? On top of that soft down blanket."

"Oh." She thought of how wonderful that would be. How warm. How—

"What are you wearing?" he asked.

She looked down at her blue flannel pajamas and had a sudden realization. "Are we having phone sex?"

"Are we?" he asked, playfully. "What are you wearing, Caron?"

They *were* having phone sex! She glanced back down at her pjs. "A pink silk gown."

"I like pink," he murmured. "Tell me about it."

Tell him about it! "Pink."

"You said that," he said, almost laughing.

"Silk."

"You said that, too."

"Right."

"Long or short?" he asked, having sympathy and guiding her.

She looked down at her flannel-clad leg. "Short. Just above the knee. Spaghetti straps. Lacy bodice. I have my space heater on so I'll be warm." She hit her forehead. What a stupid thing to say.

"I'd rather keep you warm."

"That would be nice," she said. Nice! "I mean wonderful. That would be wonderful." They both started laughing.

"One day, I vow to erase that word from your vocabulary," he teased. "Now, back to getting me in that room with you right now. What color are your panties?"

She swallowed hard, thought of the white granny panties she usually wore with a nightie and lied, "Pink like the gown." Okay. Take control here, Caron. "What are *you* wearing?"

"What do you want me to be wearing?"

"Is this a trick question?"

"No trick. I'm right there with you. What would you want me to be wearing?"

"Though I do like your suits," she said slowly, "I'd hate for you to get one of them wrinkled. I think you better take it off. All of it. Go ahead and just get rid of the boxers, too."

"Let's keep the boxers," he said.

"Let's not," she countered.

He chuckled. "Okay. I'm naked. Now, let's work on getting you that way. Take off your gown, Caron. And the panties go, too."

She hesitated. "I've never done anything like this, Baxter."

"And that turns me on, Caron. It turns me on that I'll be the first."

"The first?" Her voice cracked, her throat suddenly dry.

"To make you come over the phone. You do want to come, don't you, baby?"

She melted. Good grief, melted like snow under the hot sun. Went from icy cold nerves to a warm flush spreading over her skin. And she didn't like it. No. No. "I do," she whispered. "But Baxter. I can't do this without you here with me. Joking around and stuff was one thing. But I can't go beyond that without you here, looking into my eyes, and letting me know that you feel the same things I do. I need that. I guess it's more proof I'm not that daring bombshell you met Friday night. All I can be is me."

"All I want is you, Caron, and sooner or later, you're going to figure that out."

"WHAT COLOR ARE YOUR PANTIES?"

Sarah flipped the button to Off on the van's control panel and set the audio to mute. Their phone tap was proving a little more provocative than expected, and Fred glanced at her with those smart-ass bedroom eyes and arched a brow.

"It's clear they're done talking about relevant information," she said. Sarah was not listening to phone sex with Fred. That was almost as good as having it themselves.

He rotated his chair around to face her, and she tried not to notice how close he was. "A good agent doesn't risk missing an important detail." His arms stretched toward the dial.

"Forget it," she said, covering the dial with her hand. "We are not listening to them have phone sex. And damn it, I am a good agent, no matter what you think of me."

"I never said you weren't a good agent."

"You make your opinions known."

"Or your own insecurity makes you read them how you see fit." His lips thinned, those piercing eyes narrowing in on her face. "That could have easily been you sweet-talking with Baxter," he said. "I would have been listening then, too. What's the difference?"

Then she wouldn't be listening with Fred, but she didn't say that. "Well, it's *not* me." She quickly trudged forward in hopes of redirecting the conversation. "From the moment Baxter set eyes on Caron, and we now know that was before she ever got into costume, he was completely absorbed with her. I think he might be falling for her. And that's a good thing. It's clear he's talking to her. If we keep listening, we're bound to get a nibble of something good."

"That's not what I meant and you know it," he said. "I meant you were willing to use yourself to get near Remington."

She turned to look at him. "To score the transfer I've asked for and get away from you and your superior attitude, I'd do that and more," she said. "You don't believe female agents have anything special to offer, but we do. And—"

To her utter shock, he leaned forward, elbows on his legs—his face, his body—so close, she could barely breathe. "You don't want to get away from me, and we both know it."

Fight or flight kicked in, and Sarah shifted away from him, intent on finding an exit. He gently shackled her arm, their knees colliding, heat ripping through her limbs, evil in its declaration of her desire for this man. The one she should hate. The one she did hate. "Let go."

He stared at her, unblinking, intense. "My sister was an agent."

"What?" she gasped, shocked at the declaration. "Was?" A bad feeling settled in her stomach.

"She died," he said. "The night before Christmas almost a year ago."

He let her go, recoiled away, and faced the blank television monitor.

She wanted to reach for him, started to and hesitated, her hand falling to her lap. "How?"

He scrubbed his jaw. "She was undercover, on a narcotics case, dating a guy high up in the organization.

They delivered her body to the back door of the local FBI office with a note—'She was good, but not that good.'"

Sarah froze. "I'm sorry, Fred. I—I had no idea."

"She was all I had. She'd followed in my footsteps."

"It wasn't your fault," Sarah whispered, feeling the waves of pain washing off him.

He cut her a sharp, sideways look. "I'm your partner," he said, his tone angry, hard. "I can't stop you from making dangerous choices. Don't expect me to be agreeable when you do."

The attraction between them had always been obvious, but always before she'd discounted it because he was a jerk. Only now, he wasn't so much of a jerk. And she didn't know what to do about it. So she stuck to duty. "A good agent uses their assets to be successful."

"Because the job demands that they do so, not because the agent is trying to prove something."

Indignant, she objected, "I'm not trying to prove anything!" Though deep down, she knew she was. A detective father who'd wanted a son and got a daughter. A stepbrother who'd taken the place by his side that she should have had. A string of agents who'd made her feel second best.

She sensed Fred's piercing gaze seeping right into her soul, seeing the truth. "Yes. You are. About being a female and an agent. Just like my sister was. If you have something to prove, do it outside the job where you won't get one, or both of us killed." He didn't stay for a response. "I'm going out to smoke."

"I hate it when you smoke."

"Exactly why I'm going to do it."

She huffed and focused on the blank monitor. "Damn, the man," she murmured. She couldn't stand him. So why did she want to storm after him, stomp out his damn, stinky cigarette, and then kiss him until the pain she saw in his eyes disappeared?

She flipped on the audio, hoping like heck that the phone sex was over because she knew without a doubt that right now, she couldn't take hearing two people who were falling in wild, passionate love. Because they were. Baxter Remington and Caron Avery were falling in love. While she and Fred seemed to be falling apart.

"Happy Holidays, Sarah," she muttered.

The audio filled the room. "Good night, Caron."

"Good night, Baxter."

The line went dead. Caron's sigh followed, a soft, satisfied sound that had Sarah wondering just how good that phone sex must have been. Her attention went to the van doors where Fred had exited. And she wondered just how good he would be. Wondered if she dared find out. Maybe she'd celebrate her transfer by finding out. But until then, he was her partner, and he was hands-off.

Maybe she'd have to find out sooner. Maybe Christmas. They'd both be alone. They'd both be in need of comfort, and she found herself wanting to give it to him, for reasons she didn't dare allow herself to consider. It would be one night. Only one night. And unlike Caron Avery, Sarah knew how to count. One night would be one night. No exceptions. No complications. Just pleasure.

# *13*

IT WAS TEN O'CLOCK ON Friday morning when Caron settled into her office chair, smoothing her navy blue skirt over her knees, just above her boots. Her matching turtleneck was warm enough that she could shrug off her light jacket. She was eager to dig into last-minute prep for the weekend holiday sale. And despite the few hours of sleep—having stayed up talking on the phone with Baxter until 3 a.m.—she barely contained a smile. Especially considering it was one of several nights in a row they'd talked almost until dawn.

She'd never talked to a man on the phone for so long, but the time had flown by with Baxter. Hearing him talk about his past, his present, even his future hopes, intrigued her immensely. And when he'd prodded her into talking about her life, she'd found herself surprisingly willing. Perhaps because the more she learned of his family, the more she recognized their rise to the top hadn't been spun with silk and satin, but rather built with hammers and nails, like hers.

This evening, Baxter would return home, and though admittedly she had a fluttery nervous feeling in her stomach, she couldn't wait to see him. Another first for her because she didn't remember any man ever making her feel that way. But then, she hadn't really dated all that much. No one had really made her feel dating was much more than drama. Until Baxter.

Intent on a little caffeine boost, Caron headed for the kitchen, where she'd left the gorgeous gift basket, compliments of Baxter, filled with coffee, chocolate and all kinds of goodies from the Remington stores—a thank-you for the "Two-Hour Dash" idea, with a note saying he'd thank her "properly" in person.

Kasey appeared in the doorway of the kitchen about the time Caron filled her mug. At the same moment, her cell phone started to ring as it lay on the counter.

"Don't get that," Kasey ordered. "Not yet."

With a frown, Caron agreed, "Okay." She set her coffee down beside the demanding phone. A sense of something being wrong told her to steel herself for a jolt as she urged Kasey onward. "What's happening? What's wrong?"

Kasey hesitated and then asked, "Have you seen the paper?"

"No," Caron replied. "I didn't have time this morning." She'd slept in to compensate for being up so late on the phone.

Kasey pulled the paper from behind her back and dropped it on the counter. "Page twelve. There is a long piece about Baxter Remington's VP and Baxter's role in the whole mess. Then the article goes on to trash his personal life. They talk about you, Caron. They say he's dating you. That suddenly he's discarding his blonde bimbos for a 'good girl' and that the timing's quite the coincidence." She narrowed a knowing stare on Caron. "Never mind what the article says. That day he came in here… I told you, I saw how he was looking at you. This newspaper story means nothing. Baxter Remington digs you. The man is into you."

Caron's head was aching and her stomach wasn't much better. She grabbed the paper along with her other items. "I need a few minutes alone."

Kasey stepped aside, having the good sense to quickly clear the path for Caron's departure. Caron's cell phone started ringing again. She eyed the caller ID. Baxter. Of course. He'd read the paper. The whole world probably had, except her. And she didn't want to. She'd heard enough from Kasey.

Part of Caron wanted to take the call, to hear Baxter tell her the article was untrue, because hearing it from Kasey had soothed a tiny bit of the bite. Hearing it from Baxter would probably help more. Or would it? Another part of her felt hurt and betrayed, for probably illogical reasons, but still hurt and betrayed. It didn't matter that the press, not Baxter, had done this. It felt bad, whether that was fair to Baxter or not.

Caron entered her office, shut her door and leaned against the wall, her attention fixed on the red-and-pink-wrapped package on the corner of her desk—the gift for Baxter's sister. She pushed off the wall and all but fell into her chair. Her cell phone rang again. And again.

When it finally stopped, Caron set it on the desk and pushed the voice-mail button: You have three unheard messages. Message number 1. *Caron. Call me, please. I need to talk to you.* Next message. *Caron. I keep calling, and you're not answering. I have to assume you saw the paper. Please, Caron. Call me. Don't let this get to*

*you. This is what the press does. This is—* Next
message. *Caron. I'm crazy about you. I can't wait to see
you tonight. Please. Don't let the press get to you. I have
to hang up. I'm going through security at the airport.
I'll call—*

Yes, she knew he'd call again soon and she had to
decide what she was going to do about it. How to deal
with the conflicted emotions eating her up inside. And
she didn't have much time to think before that next call
would come. He was taking an early-morning flight to
St. Louis to do store inspections and then flying home
later in the day. She knew all of this because he'd told
her while he'd been planning their time together for this
evening. Time that she wouldn't be sharing with him
after all.

Caron squeezed her eyes shut. She couldn't do this.
Everything was out of control. There was no way to
plan, no way to structure it all so that it could be controlled and that included what she was feeling. She was
falling for Baxter in a really big way, and she could tell
she was going to get hurt. Or hurt him. Everyone
wanted to use her against him.

She needed to get back on task—focus on her
business, on paying back her grandmother. That needed
to be her primary goal. Not wading around in the
recesses of broken heart syndrome and earning bad
press for the store and for Baxter. *People might feel
sorry for you, Caron. Come and buy from you because
you're so pathetic.* That thought was an absolutely de-
pressing one.

She eyed the beautifully wrapped present and knew
she had to get it to Baxter. Using a delivery person

would be smart and easy, but she quickly discarded that option. She wasn't about to allow a note to potentially end up in the wrong hands—like those of the press, or even the FBI. Taking the package herself gave her the opportunity to leave the key and a note, though it opened her up to being followed.

The timing for her and Baxter was horribly wrong. The world was spinning, and she had to make it stop.

AS EXPECTED, BAXTER had called her cell phone several more times throughout the day, but Caron didn't talk to him. She'd stuffed her phone in her purse and forced herself not to check the messages. And now, hours later, with the heavy birthday present pushed into a shopping bag for easy carrying and discretion, Caron headed down the hall toward Baxter's apartment. It was far too close to his arrival time to suit her comfort level, but the store had been swamped with customers and getting away had been difficult. It seemed every nosy female in the city, and quite a lot of men wanted to know who Baxter's "good girl" was. Remarkably, all that curiosity had translated into a flood of purchases and praise for the store, and Alice had rushed in after class to help manage the register.

So finally, near eight, only an hour before Baxter was set to arrive home—having received a nod from security as being on some clearance list—Caron slid the key into his front door.

She made it unnoticed along the corridor and shut the door, the sound of holiday music touching her ears. Oh, God. Was Baxter home and she didn't know it? Why hadn't she listened to the messages? She turned to the door to exit. Turned back. No. She would not be a coward. Well, that had been the plan, but not now that she was here. Think. Okay. Right. Think.

Caron set the package on a foyer table of black glass. That seemed a start. Then she drew a breath and took the stairs before she chickened out, rounding the corner to bring the living room into view—and froze. Or her feet did. Her heart charged into a wild patter, adrenaline forced through her blood in a blast of shock at what she saw. Standing next to a Christmas tree that hadn't been there before, was a blonde female, busily decorating it and humming to the "Winter Wonderland" song that was filling the air. And not just a blonde, but a bombshell in high heels with curves to die for, shown off under a snug red dress. Caron turned, this time in flight, and ran smack into the hard chest of Baxter.

"Oh, no," she said, her hands pressed to that impressive wall of muscle.

"Oh, yes," he rebutted. "Why haven't you been taking my calls? I was about to come to the store to get you."

Huh? Her gaze rocketed to his. "But you've had your hands a little *full,* I see. Or maybe a lot full! You jerk!"

"What?" he asked, his dark brows dipping. And damn him, he smelled all masculine and wonderful, and she hated him for it.

"You heard me," she blasted. "Jerk!"

"Is this Caron?"

The female voice came from behind her; she was stunned that the woman knew her name. "Did she just ask if I'm Caron?"

Baxter stared down at her, his eyes lighting with sudden understanding of her assumption. "Caron," he said softly. "Meet Rebecca. My *sister.*"

"Your…" She couldn't seem to form the words. "Your…yo…"

"Sister."

Caron whirled around and took in the blonde bombshell. Baxter's hands settled possessively, warmly, on her shoulders. The woman was blonde. But Baxter had dark hair! Caron inwardly cringed. Marilyn wasn't really blonde, either. Damn. "Hi," Caron said, waving an awkward hand.

"I am Rebecca, Caron." She smiled a sly smile that said she knew what was going on. "And you're right. He can be a jerk every now and then. Make sure you keep calling him on it, too. Too few do." She rushed forward and offered her hand. "So nice to meet you."

Caron slipped her hand into Rebecca's, noting that same appealing sparkle in Rebecca's eyes that Baxter possessed. "Nice to meet you."

Rebecca waved her forward. "Come chat with me while I decorate."

Caron turned and glanced up at Baxter, warmth spreading through her limbs the minute her eyes met his. Her hand itching to reach up and touch the shadowy jaw that told of a long day of travel. His tie was gone, the top button of his dark blue shirt undone. He looked good, and being near him felt good. How could she simply walk away from this man?

His brow arched, dared her to decline his sister's invitation. Not that Caron really wanted to. Despite her earlier intention to leave his life, she was intrigued by

Rebecca, and wanted a chance to learn more about Baxter.

Caron followed Rebecca to the corner near the fireplace, opposite the bar, memories flooding her mind about her and Baxter's lovemaking right there in that room.

"Baxter has been telling me all about your store," Rebecca said, reaching for an ornament as Caron joined her. "I can't wait to come by." Caron glanced at Baxter, who now sat on the couch, his arms stretched out across the leather pillows behind him. He'd been telling his sister about her? His eyes met hers, dark, warm with interest.

"I'd like that," Caron responded to Rebecca, reaching for an ornament to help her decorate. "I'm very proud of it. It doesn't compare with Remington Coffee, of course—"

Rebecca touched her arm. "We started small," she said and reached for another ornament. "And frankly, I'd never want to deal with something as big as Remington is now. I'm glad Baxter does it. But look at the junk he goes through in the process. No, thank you." She looked over her shoulder at her brother, before glancing back at Caron. "Which is why my fiancé surprised me with a trip to Russia for my birthday." She eyed Baxter. "Said Baxter urged him to get me out of town, away from all of this."

"Russia!" Caron exclaimed. "Baxter told me you've been wanting to go. How exciting."

"It's very exciting," she agreed. "But we leave Monday morning and won't be back until after the New Year. That's why I had to make sure he had a tree before

I left. I know how he is. He'd have dismissed it as unimportant."

"The tree is an amazing thing for you to do." And Caron meant it. She'd always had a secret desire to have a sibling who would look out for her.

Rebecca smiled her appreciation and turned to Baxter. "She's absolutely charming." She laughed. "Not at all one of those blonde bimbos like me that the paper referred to." She made a face. "Good grief, you'd think if a woman is blonde, she can't have brains. I wanted to go kick that reporter and shove my Master's degree down his throat."

Caron blushed hot, fire touching her cheeks at the newspaper reference. "I didn't even think of that angle. He was really insulting to a lot of people."

"To women in general and certainly to my brother." Rebecca motioned Caron to the couch. "There's a certain breed of reporter who looks for anything that sells papers, and when they can't find it, they manufacture it. I know my brother. That reporter was way off base. You aren't some token 'good girl.' You wouldn't be standing here, in his home, talking to me right now, if he didn't think you were special."

"She's right," Baxter said softly, reaching for Caron's hand as she neared and pulling her to the spot right next to him. "And I would have said so myself today if you would have taken my calls."

Regret about her actions spiraled through Caron. There was a bond between her and Baxter, something she didn't doubt now that she was by his side, looking into his eyes. "I should have answered. I was upset. Admittedly, I wasn't feeling overly logical."

"Understandable," Rebecca stated, perching on the arm of the couch. "I was upset when I read the story and not just because of the way it blasted my brother's character so unfairly. I thought about being in your position and how you must feel."

"There was a bright side," Caron said, trying to shift the conversation away from an uncomfortable topic. "My store was bombarded with people. We sold books and gifts galore." She held up a finger. "Which reminds me." She glanced at Baxter and lowered her voice, "Her gift is by the door."

"I'll get it," he said, his eyes warm as they touched hers, but there was also a promise that they had to talk, to clear the air. And she wanted to. Wanted to badly.

The minute Baxter slipped away to retrieve the gift, Rebecca lowered her voice and said, "He never talks about women, but he told me about you, Caron, and I have a good feeling about you. Don't let this junk going on around him scare you away."

The truth was, it almost had, and Caron found herself sorry for that. She didn't believe Baxter was guilty of wrongdoing in his company, nor did she believe he was guilty of what the newspaper had insinuated, not now that she was with him again. Now that she could look into his eyes and feel their connection.

More and more, it was becoming clear, Baxter stood alone as he faced this thing with Jett. He'd shielded his family, worked to protect his employees. If he needed her, she wanted to be there for him.

That didn't change the fact that she was scared about opening herself up to him, about getting hurt. But being scared hadn't stopped her from opening her store, nor had it stopped her from walking down that runway. Baxter didn't fit into her carefully laid out plans, nor did the craziness that had ensued upon his appearance in her life. But she knew now that he was worth some risk, even if it wasn't calculated.

BAXTER KISSED HIS SISTER goodbye at the door not more than an hour after Caron arrived at his apartment. Though he regretted Rebecca's holiday departure, he knew she was happily on her way to her dream trip, and he couldn't help but be eager to have Caron alone.

The instant the door shut, he sought her out. He found her in the kitchen, where she'd just retrieved two wineglasses from the rack above the counter. Baxter closed the distance between them, pulled her into his arms and kissed her. It was a punishing kiss, a kiss born of hours and hours of frustration when Caron had shut him out, refused his calls.

"You were going to leave that gift and walk away," he accused when finally he pulled away from her. He was hot and hard, ready to take her to bed and make love to her, but not like this, not with so much still unspoken. "And don't tell me you weren't."

Her lashes lowered, dark semicircles on pale ivory perfection. "Yes," she admitted, meeting his gaze. "But I was suffering from temporary stress. I freak out when everything feels out of control."

The answer, the confirmation that he was right, punched him in the gut. She'd been ready to walk away when he couldn't possibly imagine doing so. What if she still was?

Shaken, Baxter released her, stepped back and

leaned his hands on the counter. "So you were going to walk away."

"No, I—"

"You just said you were," he countered, noting the dismay on her lovely face, his gaze drawn to the long, silky brunette strands of her hair, thinking of what it would be like to have them brush his face, his chest. Damn it. He ground his teeth, refocused. "I don't know what to say or do, Caron. You were going to walk away, yet when you saw my sister here, you were jealous."

"I was *not* jealous!" she objected indignantly, her hands balling by her sides. "I was angry. I was—okay, I was jealous." She made a tiny growling sound of frustration. "If I was really going to walk away, do you think I would have brought your sister's gift to you in person? I was rattled, Baxter. Really, really rattled. I've never dealt with press and investigations and stuff like that. I like structure, planning. I like to know what to expect and when to expect it. Since meeting you, that hasn't happened pretty much ever."

He didn't move, though he wanted to. But this was another one of those moments, he knew in his gut, when he had to give her space. "I can't control much of what is going on around me right now. I want to, Caron, but I can't. So you're right. My life won't allow structure and planning. Not until this is over. Can you deal with that?"

She waved her hands a bit helplessly before saying, "Obviously, I can, or I wouldn't be standing here."

"That's not true," he reminded her. "You planned to come and go before I arrived home. You didn't expect me to be here."

"I explained that."

"Explain again."

She inhaled. Let it out. "Baxter, I like you."

"I like you, too, Caron."

"No," she said. "I like you in that scary, I-think-about-you-way-too-often, I-can't-believe-I'm-admitting-this kind of way. I—"

For a second time, Baxter reached for her and held her in his arms. "I like you in the…you-make-me-crazy-for-too-many-reasons-to-name…kind of way," he said. "And I don't know what to do about it, but I do have a suggestion."

"What's that?" she asked.

"Let's make love all night and try to work each other out of our systems."

"Didn't we try that already?" she asked, a bit breathlessly.

"Yes."

"And it didn't work."

"No," he said. "But we really enjoyed ourselves. I believe it merits one more dedicated effort."

She smiled. "I do like how you think."

# 14

IT WAS AFTER LUNCH on Sunday and rather than working in his office as usual, Baxter sat behind Caron's desk in her office, a slow Sunday afternoon weeding through the unimpressive financial reports for the prior week on his laptop. Normally, he'd be at his office, but having Caron nearby, attending her ever-flowing rush of customers, eased the pain of having to work. Actually, it made work enjoyable. There was a first. But then, there were a lot of unique things about his relationship with Caron.

After a weekend spent with her by his side, day and night, he only wanted her more. There was passion between them and not simply blazing hot sex—though there was plenty of that, but passion for shared interests, passion for conversation and healthy debate. More and more, it became clear—Caron was special. He wasn't willing to call it "love," not yet, but he wasn't willing to rule out the possibility that it might be headed there. In the most turbulent time of his life, she'd managed to be the calm in the storm, when he would have doubted anyone could be.

"I can't believe how busy it is." Caron had appeared in the office, little ringlets of dark hair fluttering around her face, the rest tucked neatly at the nape of her neck. "I guess the saying about how 'there is no such thing as bad advertising' is true."

"I don't know if I agree with that, considering my current circumstances," he commented, but despite the slightly embittered tone of his remark, he felt his mood lighten as she walked around the desk and leaned on the wooden surface beside him.

He shoved the chair back and rotated to frame her body. "In your case, the charity event promotion was hefty and then followed up by the article, you were well-exposed. And not just to me," he teased, "though that was the best part in my book." His hand settled on her leg, her slim black skirt covering her knee beneath his palm. She had a classy, sleek way of dressing that he admired, though he was damn thankful today for his Sunday-casual jeans and shirt. "Seriously though. I'm happy your sales are up. You deserve to get something out of all of this. And even when the rush dies down, you'll maintain growth."

Her hand slid to his as she shyly said, "I am very happily exposed, thank you very much. To you, Baxter." There was no mischief, no sensual meaning, just the spontaneous honesty he'd come to expect from her. Too often she took him off guard as no other woman had managed to do, and the fact that she could, drove him further into the realm of no return. He wanted Caron in his life, shaking things up, making him crazy wondering when she would surprise him again.

He took her hand. "Caron—"

"Baxter," Kasey interrupted from the door. "There's a call on two for you. The guy refused to say who he was. Want me to get rid of him?"

His eyes met Caron's, the silent message that both were aware anyone calling him on the store phone wouldn't be good news. "Reporters," Caron ground out. "I wish they'd leave us alone."

She was probably right, but Baxter's instincts clamored with the promise of something more. "I'll take care of it, Kasey."

"Okay," Kasey said. "And Caron. I have a woman asking for ten of the romance bags, and we don't have them. Can you work some kind of magic and produce them or do I tell her no?"

Caron hesitated, obviously torn between finding out what the call was about and helping Kasey. He kissed her hand. "Go. Make the sale. I've got this."

Reluctantly, she nodded. "Let me know if there is trouble. I'll call the police."

"You just focus on your store," he said. "I'll deal with the trouble, if there is any."

Baxter grabbed the line as she exited the office and gave his standard greeting. "Baxter Remington."

Jett's muffled voice came through the line. "Pay phone at 5th and Levine in ten minutes." The phone went dead.

Baxter had expected him to call again, but not until the eleventh hour, sometime Monday. And he'd prepared for it. Things were simply moving a little faster than expected.

He quickly pushed to his feet, shut his computer and slid it into his briefcase. Baxter had a pretty good idea where this call was leading, and action would be required. Unwilling to expose Caron to any further nastiness until it was done and over, and knowing she wouldn't allow him to shelter her, he tore off a piece of paper from a nearby pad and grabbed a pen.

Taking care of a problem before it becomes bigger. I'll be away a few hours. Don't worry. Meet you at your place at eight. I'll bring dinner.

He set the note in the center of the desk, hating that he had to leave her like this, but knowing it was the right thing. He shoved his arms into the leather jacket he'd hung over the chair and gave the note another glance, unhappy with how abruptly it read. He grabbed the pen and added,

I'm crazy about you every second I'm with you, Caron.

And then, before he ended up having to explain things to her face-to-face, he made a fast exit out the back door and straight to the pay phone.

Baxter paced as he waited for the line to ring. He picked it up the minute it did, not bothering with hello, and heard, "Your VP ending up in prison isn't going to help the reputation of the company."

No more denials of guilt, Baxter noted and replied, "I've considered that." Less than a minute later, the call ended, and Baxter had an agreement in place with Jett—one that sat as easily as heavy bricks on his chest.

He started walking, pressing buttons on his cell. "It went down as planned."

The voice on the other end said, "I'll advise the necessary contacts and be in touch shortly."

IT WAS WELL PAST DINNERTIME, and there was still no sign of Baxter. Caron sat on her navy blue well-worn couch and read the letter from Baxter for at least the tenth time. She'd long ago traded in her skirt for sweat suit and bare feet, determined to go to bed unaffected by Baxter's absence. Right. Unaffected by Baxter was a joke.

Curling her legs onto the cushion, she didn't know if she should be mad or worried. She didn't want anything to be wrong with him, but she didn't want him to be an insensitive jerk who didn't deserve all the angst he'd created in her. She'd never been in a relationship that had twisted her in knots to the magnitude of this one, that made her feel the fear of rejection. It scared her.

Yet, when she was with Baxter, she felt happier than she'd ever imagined possible with a man. She'd always recognized the risk-and-reward aspect of dating, just never found anyone worth the risk. She didn't want today to be the day Baxter proved he had been a mistake. She didn't want that day to come—ever.

Determined to stop making herself crazy, Caron put the letter away and grabbed the television remote. She was about to punch the on button when a knock sounded on the door. More eager than she'd like to admit, even to herself, she discarded the remote and rushed toward the door, forgetting caution, and yanked it open.

There stood Baxter, his arm over his head, leaning on the door frame, his hair rumpled and sexy. His eyes dark, face etched with strain. "God, you look good," he said, and before she knew what was happening, he was in the foyer, wrapping powerful arms around her and walking her backward.

"Baxter—"

He kissed her, kicking the door shut at the same time, and drugging her with sensual strokes of his tongue. Somehow, she managed to drag her lips from his, her hands pressed to the solid wall of his chest. "I was worried."

Turbulent eyes met hers. "I couldn't call," he said. "I'll explain everything, I promise." His hands framed her face. "Right now—right now, I just need you, Caron."

The force of the emotion in his voice, etched in his face, in his eyes, set aside any hesitation in Caron. His hunger seeped through her resistance, tore a hole in her will-power. She believed him. Believed he would explain and believed he needed her. "I'm here," she whispered hoarsely, a moment before his mouth slanted over hers again.

She clung to him, realizing that the fear she'd felt had been about losing him, about never again feeling this wild burn that only he created in her. Afraid that he affected her more than she did him. But she knew better, knew in every inch of her body, every corner of her soul, that he felt what she felt. Something powerful was happening between them, and she didn't have the will to fight it.

He turned her, pressed her against the wall, her hands flat against the wooden surface. A wildness radiated from him, through his actions, that had her gasping for air, aroused to the point of panting. His hands slid over her hips, heavy, possessive. She could feel the warm, wet heat, gathering in the V of her body, arousal thrumming a path through her limbs.

His breath touched her ear, his hand wrapping around her, covering her breasts and kneading. "Tell me you want me."

"You know I do," she assured him.

"Say it," he ordered, his hands sliding under her T-shirt—she was braless, her nipples throbbing even before his fingers tugged them with delicious insistence. "Say it."

"I want you," she gasped.

He rolled and tweaked her nipples. Pleasure shot through her limbs, darting to her core. She tried to shut her legs, tried to do anything to ease the ache there. Baxter was having no part of that, his knee holding her thighs apart, easing her wide again. His hands slid inside her sweatpants, and he took her off guard when he instantly tried to ease them down her hips.

Caron panicked, tried to turn. The idea of being naked in her tiny corridor with Baxter standing over her fully dressed was intimidating, despite all they had done together. But there was no turning, no resisting. Baxter held her easily. "You want me," he said against her ear. "But do you trust me?"

"Yes," she said. "I trust you."

His hands slid over her hips, over her backside. Her legs were weak. "Then just let go, Caron. Just be with me and forget everything else."

She closed her eyes shut, his words reaching inside her and touching her in places well beyond erotic. Just be with him. She wanted to. Yes. She wanted someone in her life she could simply be with, no need for barriers, no need for nerves or caution.

"I want that," she replied honestly. "I want that so much."

His lips brushed her ear again, nibbling. Skilled hands explored her body, touched her, caressed her, until he turned her to face him, lifting her and carrying her the few steps to her tiny kitchen before setting her on the counter.

His hands slid down her legs, spread them. He stepped closer and she wrapped her arms around his neck as he pressed his cock to the V of her body. He was thick with arousal and the wanton woman that she'd become since meeting him wanted to tear open his pants, impatient to have him inside her. Instead, she was drawn into a long, passionate kiss. And another.

They nipped, they tasted, licked. She wasn't sure who was wilder. Him or her. Wasn't sure which one of them decided her T-shirt would end up on the floor. Or which one decided his would follow. The not knowing was the part that felt so liberating. For once, she wasn't thinking. For once, all she knew was the lift of her hips as her pants came down, the erotic pleasure of him spreading her wide again and staring down at her with pure, white-hot lust.

He stepped back and reached for his pants, but his eyes were locked on her, hot as they slid over her naked body with so much unbridled passion, her nerve endings sizzled. By the time he toed off his shoes and disposed of his clothing, she was reaching for him, crazy hot with need. And it was with complete, utter spellbound lust, that she watched as he pressed the head of his erection inside her. She could see the strain etched on his face, the desire to push into her, to take her. He was emotionally on edge, looking for a release. He was hard, so hard, and she wondered if she could take him, watching, feeling the thick width of his cock stretching her, the steely length of him inching deeper and deeper inside her. She widened her legs, wrapped them around his hips to pull him closer. He snapped with her response, as if she'd unleashed the wildness within him. The need, the burn.

He palmed her backside, tilted her hips. Caron pressed her hands into the counter, arching into him, and she knew in the past she would have clung to him, hiding her desire by burying her face in his neck. But she didn't hide. She lifted her hips, met his thrusts with pushes, her breasts bouncing with the action, his eyes scorching her with hot inspection. The feeling of being completely uninhibited, of animal lust that came from a sense of complete freedom, overcame her, aroused her. Pushed her to take more of him.

In response to her demands, his thrusts became tighter, faster, his jaw set with the desire etched in his face as he, too, strained for—more. She could see and feel how on edge he was, how close to coming, just as she herself was.

Biting her lip, Caron whispered, "More." Never before had she demanded anything during sex, but she found herself saying that word louder. "More, Baxter."

His gaze went to her, hot flames of lust blazing in the stare. He leaned over her, his hands by hers, his rock-hard, sweat-glistened body framing hers. "Did I mention, I'm crazy about you?" he whispered, his voice low and seductive.

A second later, he thrust his tongue past her lips, ravishing her mouth as he buried his cock to the hilt, jolting her with the intensity of the connection. She shivered and shook, exploding into orgasm, her muscles grabbing at him, taking him deeper. Desperate to keep him there until the last spasm ended, her legs shackled him tight as he ground out one last pump of his hips and moaned with his release. He buried his head in her neck and Caron buried her fingers in the dark, silky strands of hair.

Long moments of pleasure passed as they clung to one another. Eventually, Baxter leaned away, looking at her, as if seeking her permission. "I want to tell you what happened."

She touched his jaw. "I want to hear."

AN HOUR AFTER ARRIVING at Caron's apartment in a whirlwind of turbulent emotion, Baxter sat on the floor of Caron's living room, leaning on her couch, one of her legs stretched across his lap, a news talk show playing softly in the background. He'd tossed on his jeans and T-shirt, left his shoes somewhere near the front door. Chinese food take-out boxes sat open on the coffee table they'd used as their dining area.

"My head is spinning with everything you've told me," Caron said. "I still can't believe Jett called again. And that you're actually helping the FBI set him up. You were so resistant to the idea of him being guilty."

"I still am," he said, "but for the wrong reasons. Not because he's innocent but because I want him to be." He grimaced. "But he's not. He's not innocent."

Studying him, she asked, "When did you decide he was guilty, Baxter?"

"Wednesday night on the phone with you."

Surprise flickered across her face. "On the phone with me? How did I convince you Jett was guilty?"

"That first night talking about the plumber. You told me about that time you walked out of the store with a plunger in your hand and got to the car and realized you hadn't paid. So you walked back into the store, plunger in hand, and told them you needed to pay. Most people would have left, if for no other reason than embarrassment. But you knew that was wrong so you stayed."

She blushed. "Oh, yeah. I so wish I hadn't told you that story. Clearly, one of my rambling, saying-too-much—"

He squeezed her leg. "You didn't say too much. You said just enough. You reminded me that honest people do what's right, even when it's embarrassing or painful in some way."

"I'd hardly compare a two-dollar plunger to what Jett faces," she reminded him.

"I know that," he said. "But it made me think of little parts of Jett's personality that I should have noticed before. Ways he would cut corners at other people's expense. Plain and simple, Jett is not acting like an innocent man. He's calling me for money, not because he wants help clearing his name, but because something in his plan went wrong." The truth sat in his gut like acid. "And I did what I think is right. I called my attorney and prepared to take action."

"You were that sure Jett would call back?"

"Yeah," he said. "There was a desperate quality to his voice that night at the restaurant that seeped through his words. The more I replayed the call in my mind, the more I recognized it."

"But he didn't call until today," she pointed out. "That doesn't seem desperate."

"He might be desperate, but he didn't want to *seem* desperate. That was why I was surprised when he called when he did. I didn't think he'd call until tomorrow, the exact day of my deadline."

"This whole thing makes me nervous," she said. "Desperate people do desperate things. You don't know when or where you are meeting him, just that he will call, and you're supposed to give him money. What if he sees you as a risk—what if he lashes out at you in some way."

Baxter kissed her hand. "I'll be fine." But damn it felt good to have her worry, to know he had someone here for him he could actually talk to about this. "The fact that the FBI is nervous means they'll be careful." Memories of a long afternoon with them came wearily to mind. "Believe me. After hours of being drilled and rehearsed for any possible outcome of tomorrow's call, I know how nervous they are and how careful."

"But are *you* nervous?"

"Real men don't get nervous," he said jokingly.

She shook her head. "I'm serious, Baxter. Are you nervous?"

"As hell," he admitted.

Seconds passed with her studying him, before she softly said, "I'm sorry about Jett."

He touched her cheek, brushed her hair behind her ears. "Life happens."

She quickly countered his dismissal, unwilling to let him hide from the emotions he'd tried to bury. Understanding what was going on inside him, she said, "Trusting him wasn't wrong."

"Tell my stockholders that." He snorted. "Tell my father that. He never had this kind of crap happen when *he* ran the company."

"I bet he did," she scoffed. "But like you, he shouldered it on his own. Let everyone believe he was *superhuman* when he was simply *human*. And you've never once mentioned him being upset. In fact, you've referred to how amazingly supportive of you he's been."

"He has been," Baxter agreed. "But I can't get rid of that gut-wrenching feeling, of being the one at the helm of his creation while it's stumbling."

"Good people do bad things, Baxter," she said, turning to lean against the coffee table to face him. "You have no idea what drove Jett to do this and may never know, but you didn't do this. He did. The stock will recover as soon as it's clear this is under control. And you're getting it under control."

Baxter felt everything inside him go utterly, completely still in the midst of one resounding thought. He trusted Caron. But he had trusted Jett, too, trusted him the way he trusted family. If she ever burned him, he didn't know what he would do.

Caron reached for a fortune cookie and handed it to him. "Open it. See what great things await tomorrow."

He laughed and cracked open the cookie, reading the tiny paper while Caron popped a piece of a cookie into her mouth. "'It takes more than good memory to have good memories.'" He shook his head. "What the heck does that mean?"

Her expression lit with mischief. "There is only one way to interpret fortune cookies properly," she said, grinning, taking the paper and tossing it on the table with the broken cookie. "It's the simplest method any high-school-age student can tell you."

He quirked a brow. "And what would that be?"

"You add the words *in bed* behind the statement. So—'It takes more than good memory to have good memories…'" Her eyes twinkled as she went on to say, "in bed."

"Leave it to you, Caron Avery," he said, reaching for her and tugging her snug against his side, "to find a way to make me smile. Shall we go try and make good memories?"

"My bed or yours?" she playfully asked. "Yours is bigger. Mine is closer. But all your clothes for an early day's work are at your place."

"I vote for both," he said. "That gives us an excuse to maybe double the memories." Caron was exactly what he needed the night before the storm that tomorrow was sure to hold.

# 15

A RINGING SOUND BROKE through the warm, deep slumber in Baxter's bedroom where Caron slept. Snuggled next to him, she awoke abruptly, the jarring ring of his cell phone nearby. Caron lifted her head. Baxter didn't move. He was completely knocked out, exhausted after a night of sleepless worry that she'd done her best to eliminate. But he'd known the hammer was waiting to strike the next day, that he would wake and be forced to face the official loss of a man he'd thought was a friend.

Caron glanced at Baxter's alarm clock next to the phone. His cell stopped ringing as she blinked at the time. "Oh, my God!" Caron touched his chest, trying to wake him. "Baxter. We overslept. It's almost nine. The alarm didn't go off."

Groggily, he lifted his head. Turned to the clock and then scrambled to a sitting position, his hair mussed, eyes wild. "Sonofabitch! I'm supposed to be at my attorney's office in thirty minutes."

His cell started ringing again. Baxter grabbed it, looked at the ID. Answered. "Hello." The call lasted all of ten seconds before he ended it, reached for the remote control and scooted up against the headboard.

He flipped on the television. The screen filled with a news report, a man being walked into a building, officials around him, cameras flashing.

*Jett Alexander, vice president of worldwide operations for Remington Coffee, who fled amidst charges of insider trading, and under the threat of federal prosecution, has turned himself in. This news comes with the unconfirmed reports that Alexander has a plea bargain to turn state's evidence against the president and CEO of Remington, Baxter Remington.*

"Oh, my God," Caron whispered.

"Fuck!" Baxter hit the off button on the remote and flung the device to the end of the bed. His hands were in his hair as he tilted his head downward in a moment of frustration. "Fuck!"

Caron reached for him, but he threw the covers aside and got up before she could. In bare feet, pajama bottoms and no shirt, he began pacing. He turned to her. "How *the hell* can this be happening? Do you know what this will do to our stock?"

"I do," she said, trying to sound calm when she felt anything but.

He motioned to the television, the set of his jaw hard, strain etched in his face. "Investors will react before they know the facts." The cordless house phone by his bed starting ringing again and he ignored it. "Like the fact that I am completely innocent. I cannot believe I would be accused of such a thing. That sorry, low-life bastard." The cordless stopped ringing and almost immediately started again. "My parents always call the home line. That has to be them. I don't even know what to say to my father."

"I'm sure they're worried," she said.

"I know. I know. I need to talk to them." He glanced at the cell phone ID as it began to ring, as well. Caron felt as if her ears were on permanent ring.

"My attorney," Baxter said. He answered, "What the hell is going on, Kevin?"

Caron couldn't feel more helpless. All she could do was sit and try to make out part of the conversation, which was short and apparently not so sweet. "I have to be at his office as soon as possible," he said, heading toward the shower.

The house phone rang again at the same time as his cell. "My family," he murmured. "On both lines, no doubt." He stared at his cell and confirmed. "Like I said. My family."

He stopped in the bathroom doorway and turned back to her. "Can you grab that call and tell them I'll call them back? I have to contact some critical staff members and still manage a shower." He didn't give her time to answer before disappearing inside the bathroom.

"You want me to talk to your family?" she squeaked. "I can't talk to your family!"

He poked his head back into the room. "Please, baby. Just tell them I'm not dead or in jail. That will hold them off a few hours."

She inhaled and let it out, reached for the cordless. "Okay." It stopped ringing. "It stopped ringing!" she called out.

"It'll start again," he yelled back just before the shower came on.

He was right. It started again. For the first time since

she was about to walk down that runway, she thought she might hyperventilate. *Damn it, Caron, get it together. Baxter needs your help.* She punched the answer button on the cordless.

"Hello."

"Oh, thank goodness," came the female voice. "Caron, it's Rebecca. I'm at the airport, and I just saw the news broadcast here in the gate area. Baxter didn't answer his cell. Please tell me he's not in jail or something horrid like that."

"He's in the shower," Caron said, relieved at the familiar female voice. "Trying to get ready to go to the attorney's office. He's shaken, but okay."

"Tell him I'll meet him at the attorney's office," she said. "We're trying to get our luggage retrieved now."

"No!" Caron insisted quickly. "Please, Rebecca. Baxter will be devastated if you cancel your trip. This will get handled. By the time you land in Russia, it will be over. Please. I beg of you. Go on this trip." They went on to argue a minute or two.

Finally Rebecca said, "We fly through O'Hare. Give me your cell number, and if there isn't good news by the time I hit Chicago, I'm coming home."

Relieved, Caron offered her number and prayed there would, indeed, be good news by that time. "My parents are going to be panicked. Can you make sure Baxter calls them?"

The other line had beeped several times. "I believe they're on the line now. I'll talk to them." And so Caron spoke to Baxter's mother and father. Both on the phone at once, on separate receivers. Rather than being resistant to some strange woman talking on Baxter's behalf, they acknowledged knowing her name, and thanked her for being there for Baxter. Assuring her they would be there, too, and soon.

She'd barely hung up the line when Baxter appeared in the doorway already dressed in a black suit, fitted to perfection.

She started with the good news. "I talked your sister into still going to Russia, though if she doesn't hear good news by the time they're in Chicago, she's coming back. I gave her my number and I'll handle it. Your father wants you to call him as soon as you get on the road." She swallowed hard and then gave him the bad news. "Baxter." She hated telling him this because she knew it would upset him. "He's on his way to the airport. He's coming home and he's bringing your mother."

He ran his hand over his face, weariness in his voice. "I guess I can't blame them." He sat down on the bed and reached for his watch on the nightstand. Caron crawled over the mattress and helped him put it on. He seemed content to accept her aid, as if it were one thing he didn't have to do himself. "So much for their Christmas in Paris, away from all of this," he added softly. "It's what, two weeks away?"

"I am hoping this will be over well before the holiday." Which was in eight days, not two weeks, but she didn't see any reason to point out the shorter time frame.

"We can only hope," he agreed, and turned more fully toward her. "Caron. Baby. I have to go. There's no way I can keep you out of this. The press is going to come after you."

"I know. I don't care."

He wrapped his hand around her neck and kissed her. "I'll make all of this up to you when it's over. Take you away somewhere wonderful. We can take your grandmother, too." He tried to smile, but it didn't reach his eyes. "That is, if she likes me."

"She'll love you," Caron assured him, the strength of his nearness comforting in such an uncertain time. "I was actually going to ask you to spend Christmas with us."

"Looks like we'll be doing Christmas with my family and your grandma," he said, as if it was totally expected that they would be together.

His words rang in her ears. She was falling in love. Probably already had. And she worried for him, worried that Jett, a man so obviously devious, might have done more to destroy Baxter than he knew.

"Baxter," she said, her hand resting on his chest, over the thunder of his heart. "I know you have to put on a tough exterior for the rest of the world, for your stockholders and employees. But I want you to know, you don't have to for me. I'm here for you."

"I know, Caron. And it means more to me than I can possibly show you right now. But I will. I will."

His vow warmed her but not enough to erase the fear she felt for him, or about how this day was going to turn out.

IT WAS NEARLY FIVE, three hours into the FBI meeting he and his attorney had agreed to, when Baxter sat across from Agent Walker and her partner, Agent Ross, his nerves wearing thin.

"If you plan to arrest my client, then do it," his

attorney, Kevin Hersh, stated flatly. "This is nothing more than a fishing expedition that is bordering on harassment. You have nothing more than Jett's accusations because there is nothing more to find. And you know that. You've looked. There's not one detrimental aspect to any of this that can be attached to my client." Clearly, Kevin's nerves weren't any better than Baxter's. That was good because one thing Baxter had learned working with Kevin these past five years was that the thirty-something attorney performed best in an agitated frame of mind. Point proven when Kevin added, "Therefore, this meeting is over."

Baxter silently said a "thank you." Yes. Please. Let this hell be over.

Agent Walker pursed her lips. The woman had a major chip on her shoulder that showed in her every expression.

"You have a problem with reasonable questions, Mr. Hersh?" she asked. "Or maybe your client does?" Her attentive inspection sharpened further. "Why would that be, I wonder?"

"Reasonable questions are fine," Hersh replied drily, his chiseled features schooled into an uncompromising mask, "but they've been asked and answered several times over. Reframing the same question does not make it a new question. And might I add, Ms. Walker, your methods of interrogation have proven not only ineffective, but unethical. We all know you meant to seduce him into some great confession that didn't exist."

"There is nothing unethical about being at the same place as your client," she countered. "Unless your client has some reason to feel an aversion to the FBI."

"Give me a break, Agent Walker," Hersh stated. "You planned far more than a casual encounter with my client. You simply failed to garner his attention."

"We're done here," came the short, sharp response from Agent Ross, who'd spoken infrequently during the entire inquisition. "He can go."

Agent Ross's attention swung to Baxter, and Baxter looked straight into the depths of his stare and didn't like what he saw—the man had ghosts swimming in his eyes, deep dark secrets that told of hard times, and a harder soul.

"Don't leave town, Mr. Remington," he said. "I expect you to be available if we need you again. I'd hate for anyone else to suddenly go missing."

"I have no reason to run," Baxter said, his stare unwavering. "I've done nothing wrong."

"That's not what Jett Alexander says," Agent Walker interjected.

"We keep hearing that," Kevin rejoined. "Yet we see no proof." He leaned forward, as if he were sharing an inside secret. "You know what I think, Agent Walker? I think you jumped too soon, didn't dot your i's and cross your t's with Jett. You're afraid you don't have enough to charge him, either. Now you need someone to go down, so *you* don't." He shoved his chair back. "You have no evidence. When you get some, call us." He pushed to his feet, making the termination of the meeting final. "We're leaving."

Baxter eagerly stood, ready to run out of there. "This isn't over," Agent Walker promised, leaning back in her seat as if they weren't worth the effort to stand.

Baxter followed his attorney out of the room, neither

of them speaking until they had exited the front door of the building.

"This is all speculation on my part," Kevin said, his voice low, tight. "But experience leads me to certain conclusions." They stopped beside Kevin's BMW parked beside a meter, and he continued talking over the top of the roof. "I don't think Jett turned himself in. I think the Feds located him and brought him in. He most likely panicked under pressure and offered you on a silver platter."

"I don't see what that achieves," Baxter argued inside the car as he snapped his seat belt into place. "I'm innocent."

"Right now, all they're thinking is that losing Jett means someone's head's on the chopping block. Jett's attorneys will stall, which means the Feds' hands will be tied. They'll come at you hard and fast, trying to dig up dirt before I shut them down. But that'll be faster than they think." He glanced at his watch and turned on the car. "I'll be filing a restraining order and an injunction tonight. The courts won't let this harassment continue. You just keep a low profile, and I will make this go away."

"It's not enough to make it go away, Kevin," Baxter argued as Kevin pulled into traffic. "Everyone has to know I'm innocent or Remington is ruined." He scrubbed his jaw. "I have to appeal to the media and make myself visible." He didn't even want to know what the stock would close at today. "Do some of those high-profile interviews I've been offered. Tell my side of this."

"Going public is a weapon, but one that must be used with caution," he said. "In this case it serves us well to send the message that you aren't anywhere near intimidated by any of this. I will need to approve the format of any venue you undertake as well as the questions asked and your answers, in advance."

"Understood," Baxter said, ready, willing and able to fight back. It was time to shove back. Caron was right. Protecting himself did protect those he cared about, and she was one of those people. He wanted this over, and her in his arms, and he would do what he had to in order to see that happen.

"WHAT THE HELL WAS THAT all about?" Sarah demanded, following Fred into his office where he was already sitting behind his desk, feet kicked up, as if he owned the world—or rather her career.

"We weren't getting anywhere in there. Baxter Remington has told the same story from day one. Nothing has changed."

She wanted to scream. She all but did. "You mean you didn't want to talk about me trying to seduce Baxter Remington for evidence," she accused. "I get that you don't like it when women use their bodies for duty, but men do it, too. Undercover agents do what they have to. That's the world we live in. If you can't deal with that, you shouldn't be an agent."

Furious, she turned to leave. Fred moved with stealthlike agility, and suddenly his body was framing hers, his hand on the door above her head, stopping her from opening it.

Sarah whirled around, her back against the wooden surface, forced to look up into his face. He was close. Too close. Her body betrayed her anger, uncomfortable feminine awareness shimmering across her skin.

"Get out of my way," she hissed. They'd pretended the conversation about his sister hadn't taken place, but it was there, though she'd tried to forget it. She didn't want to like Fred, didn't want to be attracted to him. And bullying behavior such as this only reminded her why she didn't respect him. "Move!"

"There is a time to push and a time to back off. It's time to back off. You're focused on getting away from *me*. It's clouding your judgment. It's the wrong reason to make a decision."

"Your ego is bigger than I thought if you believe this is all about you," she spat back, though guilt twisted in her gut. She did want to get away from Fred, away from him before he made her do something stupid and sleep with him. That would be the kiss of death for her career. "I want a transfer, yes, and a promotion. Early this week, I applied for entry into a special terrorist unit." It was where she'd get the special training to be seen as more than just a woman. "But they want a track record, Fred, and they want results. They're watching me on this one, and I have no doubt they expect me to clean up a mess and make it right. That means, cover my tail. I can't think he's innocent, I have to know he's innocent. And I can't do that with a partner who scoffs at every step I take and treats me like a little sister he has to protect." The instant the words were out, she regretted them. She'd never meant to refer to his sister. "Oh, God. Fred. I'm sorry. I didn't mean that."

He dropped his hand and stepped away from her. "I guess we finally agree on something. We can't work together. Good luck getting that promotion and Baxter Remington. It sure as hell won't be with me as your partner." He took another step backward, motioned her toward the door. "Feel free. I finally do. I won't stand in your way anymore."

Sarah's pulse raced, unexpected pain jabbing her in the heart. She grabbed the door and opened it, couldn't get away quick enough. Tears prickled her eyes. Tears! Agents didn't cry. Damn it, she didn't cry. This was why she needed to be away from that man. He confused her, made her nuts. She swiped at her cheeks.

In more ways than one, this all felt unfair. She could seduce a perp and be respected in the morning. Falling in bed with Fred was another story. Falling in love with him—well, that would be just plain crazy.

## 16

THREE DAYS AFTER JETT had suddenly reappeared and further shaken up Baxter's life—and Caron's along with it—Caron's grandmother was officially fretting. She'd seen the news and the papers, and despite Caron's reassurances that she was fine, her grandma was on the phone for the third time that day.

Standing in her store, behind the register, phone jammed between her shoulder and her ear, Caron straightened the display on the counter as her grandma expressed more worry. "Yes, Grandma, I'll be careful," Caron said, only to have her grandmother launch into more worry-driven fretting.

Caron raised an apologetic finger as a customer approached, one of the many despite the late eight o'clock hour—their normal closing time if not for the extended holiday hours. The well-advertised, unavoidable store schedule meant that she might not make it to Baxter's in time to watch the national news show in which Baxter would appear that night. At least, not in real time at his place, with him and his parents, as he had hoped. Meeting his parents had her distracted anyway. So did the outcome of this show—how it would affect his stockholder's confidence. They'd know tomorrow, when trading started, how well he was received.

Aware that her customer was staring at her, waiting patiently, Caron gently but firmly cut off her grandmother's musings. "I love you and I'm fine, Grandma. I have to take care of a customer. I'll call you in the morning." With an affectionate exchange of goodbyes, Caron replaced the receiver on the cradle and rang up her customer's purchases.

After wishing her customer goodbye, Caron glanced at the clock again, thinking Baxter should have landed about an hour ago, flying in from New York, and she wished he would call. On the other hand, she was comfortable that he would call when he could. She didn't feel out of control or scared with Baxter. She felt safe, secure.

Glancing around her store, adorned with flickering red lights and poinsettias, Caron smiled. She really was proud of her little shop. Decorating her apartment, too, had seemed a waste since she was always here or at Baxter's. Except last night, she thought longingly.

Despite his insistence that she go with him on his trip, she'd stayed behind to tend the store. Another sign Baxter was special, she thought. She wanted to be with him, but he didn't make her feel she ceased to exist without him. Simply that she was better with him.

Twenty minutes before closing, Caron stood at the register finishing paperwork, the keys dangling in the lock, ready for departure. Instinct made her look up a second before a gasp escaped her lips as Baxter pushed through the door. In a long coat and dark suit, he rounded the counter and reached for her. Caron all but fell into those warm, wonderful arms, amazed at how much she'd needed this.

"God, I missed you," he murmured, his chin brushing her hair.

She inhaled his yummy scent and wrapped her arms around his waist, smiling up at him. "I can't believe you're here." Her eyes searched his. "Your show. You won't make it home in time to watch it with your parents."

"Actually," he said. "I brought my parents with me."

Caron's eyes went wide. "What?" He brought his parents? She was meeting his parents. Now? Here?

"They're outside waiting," he said. "I thought you might want some warning. They knew I wanted to watch the show with you, so they picked me up at the airport, and we came straight to the store."

"Outside waiting is not a warning!" Caron's fingers closed around his jacket. "Why didn't you call and warn me?"

"That would have ruined the surprise."

"For future reference, since you clearly haven't figured this out—me and surprises—not really my thing. I like to *know*." She motioned to her new black pantsuit that had proven a wrinkle-grabbing disaster. "Look how I'm dressed!"

"Baxter?" The male voice came from behind and the door jingled.

Baxter quickly whispered, "You look beautiful." He released her as his parents entered the store, one of his hands resting protectively on her lower back. "Caron. Meet my parents, David and Linda Remington."

"Hello, Caron," David said, rushing forward and

offering Caron his hand. Caron was shocked at how much he and Baxter favored each other, although gray frosted his father's full, dark hair, and lines flavored his face. He smiled at her, friendly and engaging. "So nice to finally meet you."

Finally? "It is?" she asked, surprised.

He laughed and hugged her. "Don't act so surprised," he scoffed, patting her hand and studying her. "I'm glad you told my son to look out for himself in this mess. He's always worried about everyone else. It's the same damn thing I'd been telling him, but he wouldn't listen." He winked. "Next time I want him to listen to someone, I guess I'll call you."

Shocked at how readily Baxter's father accepted her, Caron glanced at Baxter, who simply looked amused and pleased with the interaction.

His mother stepped closer and extended her hand. "I'm Linda, Caron." She was a petite redhead who managed to be elegant despite barely reaching five feet tall. "I'm so glad we'll get to watch the show with you."

"Oh, yes!" Caron exclaimed, eyeing the clock and noting that several other customers still needed attention. "It starts in five minutes. We'd better go turn on the television." She focused on Baxter. "Can you take them to my office and get it set up while I lock up?"

Kasey appeared behind the register to help a customer. "I'll take care of things," she said to Caron. "You go watch the show."

"Thank you, sweetheart," Baxter's mother said. "That is so very wonderful of you." The words rang with sincerity and true appreciation. Kasey and Caron looked at one another, and Caron realized Kasey was thinking the same thing she was—that Linda Remington was a really classy woman.

"Thank you, Kasey," Caron said. "Are you sure?"

"Positive," she answered, a twinkle in her eyes as she glanced at Baxter and back at Caron.

Piled into Caron's office, the four of them watched Baxter's interview and shared comfortable conversation. He'd been firm but likable when he'd presented the FBI's approach to the securities investigation. He'd even rolled with the punches quite nicely when surprised by viewers' call-ins, and received overwhelming public support.

An hour after the show ended, the store was empty but for Caron and Baxter, his parents having left by private car. The two of them stood in Caron's office, Baxter's arms wrapped around her waist. "My parents loved you," he said.

That pleased Caron, not because she needed their approval, but because she had genuinely liked them. "I loved them, too," she said, her hands resting on his chest, his jacket long gone. Heat seeped through the white dress shirt to her palm, and before she could stop herself, she said, "I missed you, Baxter."

His hand slid down her hair. "I missed *you,* Caron." He carefully walked her toward her desk until she scooted on top of it to sit. He claimed the chair in front of her and rested his hands on her knees. "Did you know that my father is an excellent judge of character?" he asked, surprising her with the rather unexpected question. She'd expected something a little more naughty right about now.

Caron replied, "I can see that in him." She'd noted

a shrewd intelligence in David Remington's eyes, in his observations.

Baxter's expression turned serious. "He never liked Jett."

The admission took her off guard, but it explained so much. "Why?"

"He said Jett would never look him in the eyes." Baxter laughed, bitter. "I thought Jett was simply intimidated by my father's success."

"You misjudged him," she said softly. "We're all human."

He stood up, stepped close, slid his hands into her hair. The air crackled with instant sensual tension. "What if I said I was falling in love with you, Caron?"

Her heart raced wildly, nerves charging through her body. "I'd say you better mean it because that would be a really horrible joke."

His lips lifted. "Wrong answer."

She ran her hand down his tie. "I never manage to say the right thing at moments like these, do I?" Her fingers brushed his jaw. "I'm pretty sure I'm already there, Baxter. I'm done falling. I'm—"

He kissed her then, long and passionate. Then he made love to her in her office, and not even her best romance novel–evoked fantasy came close to comparing or ever would again.

THE NEXT DAY, CARON learned the hard way that fantasies in romance novels were the only ones that came with perfectly happy endings. Her life was another story.

She arrived at work after the opening bell for trading;

Remington stock was on the rise. And Baxter's attorney had said he felt the wheels were in motion now to end the mess. He had received indications that Jett Alexander had admitted he had nothing on Baxter. The bad news—Jett was likely to get off on a technicality, though his career would be over.

Caron was actually humming a Christmas tune, debating a Christmas gift for Baxter, when she walked into her office and stopped dead in her tracks. Leaning on her desk, right where Caron and Baxter had made love the night before, was Agent Walker, her long legs stretched out in front of her, crossed at the ankles, arms at her sides.

"You might want to shut that door, Caron," she said. "We have private matters to discuss."

"We have nothing to discuss," Caron countered, balling her fists by her side.

Agent Walker held up a small tape recorder. "I'd shut that door if I were you." She hit Play and Caron's voice filled the room, "Has he called again?"

Outrage and panic overcame Caron at the sound of her private phone conversation with Baxter. "You bugged my telephone? I'll sue you. I'll—"

"You'll listen and listen well or end up in jail, Caron." She turned off the recorder. "We had court orders for everything we did, and obviously we now know that you were aware Baxter was communicating with Jett, and you didn't report him. Either you come forward and give me Baxter, or I plan to turn this on *you*."

"Me?" Caron exclaimed and then bit her tongue. She would not react. That was what this woman wanted. "I did nothing wrong," she added softly, vehemently.

Appearing almost bored, Agent Walker uncrossed her arms and legs. She set the recorder on the desk and rested her palms on the wooden surface. "Obstruction of justice, impeding a federal investigation…"

Caron was beyond angry, she was fuming, spitting mad. "Why do you want him so badly? Why?" She reined in her tone, but just barely. "You lost Jett and you need a conviction. Otherwise, you get in some kind of trouble. Well, press charges if you like. I have nothing to say to you that an attorney can't say for me and better."

Unmoving, Agent Walker said, "I like you, Caron. Don't let a guy screw up your life. You're better than that."

That was it. Caron opened the door. "Leave."

Agent Walker pushed to her feet, left the recorder. "I'll let you listen to that. Feel free to let your attorney listen, too. He or she should find it interesting." She stopped in front of Caron. "Tell me what I need to know."

"As I've told you several times before, Agent Walker—"

"Several times before?" It was Baxter, standing in the doorway, with roses in his arms, accusation burning dark in his eyes. "When have you talked to her before this, Caron?"

Caron's heart lurched. He looked handsome. Angry. One step from gone. Her mind raced, her throat froze. She would have told him all of this, but it had never seemed relevant, always like past history. Done before they were even started. Something else to worry him, over nothing. "Baxter—"

"You know what," he said, cutting her off with unfamiliar coldness and chilling her to the bone. "There isn't a good answer, Caron. Not one good answer you can give me. I trusted you—the woman who told me to protect myself and was stabbing me in the back at the same time. Well, I am protecting myself. By getting away from you."

"You really think that little of me?" she demanded, but he'd already turned away, tossing the flowers on the floor as he left.

He did think that little of her. He had no intention of hearing her out. Not now. Not ever. She'd lost him. And why did she want him if he thought she'd betrayed him? Caron fought the tears that threatened to overwhelm her. Because she did still want him, damn it; and with emotion about to strangle her, she couldn't begin to reason herself out of it.

"This changes nothing, Caron," Agent Walker said, reminding Caron the woman was still there.

"Leave!" she yelled, pointing toward the empty doorway. "Leave!" Actually yes, this changed something—it had changed everything.

Baxter was gone. Caron now faced the reality that her books had allowed her to escape—fairy tales *were* fiction.

# *17*

SARAH SAT IN HER OFFICE in the San Francisco FBI hub late afternoon on Christmas Eve, a bottle of antacids on her desk that eased the knots in her stomach, but did nothing for her turbulent mood. Fred had been gone for days, having taken a leave of absence, and Jett would most likely be headed home before the night was out—free as a bird on a technicality.

Popping another milky pink tablet, Sarah stared at the manila envelope that had been delivered by a courier a few minutes earlier. Unless it gave her something to do besides go home alone, which was unlikely on Christmas Eve, she didn't want whatever was inside. Clinging to the hope that the contents might offer a needed distraction from her Christmas Eve blues, Sarah broke the seal and thumbed through the paperwork inside.

Stunned at what she'd found, Sarah sat back in her chair. "We got him. Finally, we got him."

"We" being her and Fred. Since it was Fred's hard-headed insistence that somewhere in Jett's background they'd find another misstep. Sure enough, before Jett had joined the Remington management staff, he'd played this same game of stock manipulation in another company. Jett couldn't be charged for his most recent activity, but he wouldn't walk on his past mistake.

Emotions charged at Sarah, fierce in their intensity. The same emotions she'd been suppressing, the ones eating away at her stomach. She shoved away from her desk, took the envelope with her. She had to deal with Jett before she could deal with her own personal meltdown. She wasn't about to give him a chance to run again.

NIGHT HAD FALLEN by the time Sarah pulled her Buick Skylark to a stop in front of the two-story apartment building that Fred called home. Noting his Jeep by the curb, she let out a shaky breath. He was home—like her, with no family, no holiday bliss to escape to.

But she didn't know what to say, what to do. Even why she'd come. Time ticked by as she sat there, a black hole spiraling around her as she ticked off all her mistakes these past few weeks, all the reasons she had to feel guilty. How long she sat in that car, she didn't know. Too long.

"Just go knock," she whispered, and shoved open the car door before she changed her mind.

Taking the stairs to Fred's floor, Sarah's pace was steady, rapid—with her decision made to move forward, she wasn't backing out. Nor did she hesitate at his door, knocking immediately. Almost instantly, it flew open and Fred stood in the doorway, shirtless, low-slung jeans showing off rippling, hard-earned muscles.

"Wondered how long you were going to sit in the car," he said drily.

Relief washed over her—relief that this man was once again giving her shit. That he was here, and acting as if nothing had changed. Relief that triggered the emotional meltdown she'd held off for hours. Sarah fell into his arms and started to cry.

"I didn't mean to say that about your sister," she whispered into his chest. "I didn't mean to. I'm sorry."

"I know," he said, hugging her in the warm cocoon of his arms. Warm and wonderful, accepting not rejecting. She went blank for long minutes, tears shaking her body, her emotions so long contained. Quickly, she was inside his apartment, the door shut. Then she was on his couch, sitting snug against his side.

When finally she calmed, his fingers lightly brushed hair from her eyes. "Better now?" he asked gently, no sarcasm, no anger. No walls.

"We got Jett," she said. "Or you did. You were right. He had a past. A bad one."

"I thought that would be *good* news," he said, studying her. "Not something to cry about."

"You were right about my decisions, Fred. Right about so many things. I made the wrong choices for the wrong reasons. I didn't want the agency to think I was weak because I didn't go after Remington. I wasn't confident enough to just say I knew he was innocent. And I did, I do—I know he's innocent." She went on to tell Fred about the confrontation with Baxter and Caron. "See? I really screwed this all up. I destroyed their relationship. I destroyed our partnership. I've dropped my transfer request, Fred. Please come back. We are good together. We stopped Jett."

He stared down at her, didn't blink, didn't move. "Are you sure? What about your promotion?"

She didn't want it anymore. She'd wanted it for all

the wrong reasons. "We make good partners," she repeated simply, and barely had the words out before Fred kissed her, a kiss that told of passion to come, passion barely restrained. But she couldn't allow herself the pleasure. Couldn't allow herself the peace.

Fred stopped abruptly, stared down at her. "What's wrong?"

"I destroyed their relationship," she whispered.

"Caron Avery and Baxter Remington?"

She nodded, emotion tightening her chest.

"Let's go," he said, pulling her to her feet and reaching for the T-shirt he'd flung over the edge of the couch, tugging it over his head.

"Where?"

"To see Baxter Remington." He wrapped his arm around her waist, leaned that hard body into hers. "Then we'll come back here, and you can be my Christmas present."

STANDING IN THE DEN of his parents' waterfront home, Baxter stared into the crackling fire of their white-rock hearth, a glass of brandy in his hand, Caron on his mind, no matter how hard he tried to stop thinking about her. Though pleased that his middle sister had arrived an hour before, he'd been equally as pleased when she and his mother had retreated to the kitchen for girl talk. He needed the alone time to clear his head.

"I liked her, you know."

Baxter turned to see his father in the doorway. "I know you did," he said. Looking back, he now wished he had waited to introduce Caron to his parents. "That doesn't change what she did."

"Which was what?" David Remington asked, moving to stand next to his son, staring into the same fireplace.

Baxter cast him an incredulous look. "She should have told me about being approached."

"Perhaps," he agreed, and then peered at his son, clearly concerned. "But from what I understand, even from you yourself, she told them nothing."

"She didn't tell me, Dad," he argued, frustrated, running a hand through his hair. "Didn't. Tell. Me. What part of that rings okay with you?"

"The part where she endured a beating by the press and stuck by your side. The part where she encouraged you to protect yourself and apparently did so herself, as well. That earns her the benefit of the doubt in my mind. I thought it would for you, too. But then, maybe I was wrong, and these things don't matter."

"Wrong?" Baxter asked, glancing at his father, sensing he was being led into one of his father's all-too-knowing observations.

Shrewd eyes fixed on Baxter. "I thought you were in love with her."

Baxter inhaled a harsh breath at his father's directness. His statement touched on the core of the turmoil tearing him in two.

Baxter had been in love with Caron. Damn it, he still was. But it didn't matter; he couldn't let it matter. "Secrets and lies do not equal love," he said, repeating what he had said to himself too many times to count. Jett had burned him. But finding out Caron had been talking to the FBI had cut like a knife.

"Honey."

His mother's voice had Baxter and David turning to the doorway, where she stood in her festive red velvet holiday dress. "Which honey?" Baxter's father joked.

Linda looked at him with mock reprimand. "You know I'm not talking to you, *darling.*" She refocused on Baxter. "Agents Walker and Ross are here to see you." Baxter was about to tell her to send them away, when she added, "I really think you want to hear what they have to say."

Something in his mother's voice blasted away Baxter's refusal. He downed the brandy in his glass, and set it on the hearth. "Send them in."

Agents Walker and Ross appeared moments later, minus his mother, and Agent Walker quickly launched into conversation. It only took a few minutes before he learned that he was free and clear—no more visits from the FBI.

"Thank you for that good news," Baxter said.

Agent Walker hesitated. "I approached her the morning after you met," she said, not bothering with Caron's name. "I pressured her hard. Did my best to intimidate her. She gave me nothing. And I mean nothing. Shut me off faster than flipping a light switch. That day in her office, I even played a taped conversation that proved we had good reason to suspect that you had talked to Jett. I threatened to prosecute her. She was willing to risk that. She didn't even blink before she demanded I leave. Why didn't she tell you? I don't know. But I'd heard enough, and observed enough, to know that the woman was certain that every day of your relationship would be the last. That it was a fling, and you'd soon find a real blonde bombshell. Don't prove her right. I was an ass to you and to her. Don't *you* be a fool." She said nothing more, silently turning and leaving, Agent Ross by her side.

Baxter stood there, unable to breathe. Caron hadn't betrayed him and, indeed, he was a fool. He'd let Jett and his betrayal taint his objectivity. He was crazy about Caron. He was in love with Caron.

His father's hand came down on his shoulder. "Go get her, son."

"I plan to." Baxter was already on the move and in his car in a matter of seconds. He dialed the bookstore as he pulled onto the road, aware that Caron had stayed open late for last-minute shoppers and hoping to catch her. No answer. He dialed again. No answer. He considered calling her cell, but decided this was something better done face-to-face anyway.

He screeched into the parking lot but swore again when he found Caron's car absent. But Kasey's white Camry was there, and he rushed to the back door and pounded. Nothing.

"Kasey, it's Baxter." Damn. He ran around the building to the front. Knocked on the window over and over, until Kasey finally appeared.

She unlocked the door. "You just missed her. She's gone straight to Sonoma."

"What route?"

"She takes 101 to 37."

He was already walking away as Kasey called out, "It's about time you came to your senses."

Baxter waved a hand in understanding. She was right. It was about time. And he was more than willing to spend a lifetime making up for it.

WITH HER HEART HEAVY, Caron drove toward Sonoma, thankful the day was behind her. The store had been packed; the customers arriving one after another. And they had been godsends, distractions from the growing ache of hearing nothing from Baxter. There had been a few moments of weakness, when she'd considered calling him. At other times, she called him all right— a jerk, a rich, snotty, arrogant… Well, the list went on. In the end, she didn't think he was any of those things, but she acknowledged it had felt good to lash out. In the end, he was simply a man betrayed by a close friend, fearful of being betrayed again. She should have told him, she supposed, about the FBI, but beating herself up about her logic didn't help matters.

For now, she simply wanted to get to her grand-mother's place. To drink hot cocoa and eat her grandma's famous brownies—perhaps a few dozen or so would make her feel better. She began to fantasize about those sweet treats when the car behind her flashed its lights.

"Everyone is in a hurry," she mumbled, and changed lanes to let the car pass. But the car didn't pass—it flashed its lights again. Caron frowned.

She dug her cell from the empty drink holder where she'd stashed it, preparing to call for help—just in case. It started to ring. She didn't dare take her eyes off the road, punching the answer button. "Hello."

"It's Baxter, Caron."

Her heart jackknifed. "Baxter?"

"Pull over, baby. The sign says there's a rest stop at the next exit."

"That's you behind me?"

"Yeah," he said. "It's me."

Caron started shaking and tears pricked at her eyes. Emotion overcame her; that valued control she so loved, gone. Baxter was here? On the highway? She could barely drive the half mile it took to get to the rest stop and pull into a parking spot.

It was seconds before Baxter was at her open door, dropping to his knee on the ground beside her as she turned to face him, her feet on the pavement. His hands went to her knees in that familiar way he always touched her, the wind caressing his dark hair, her nostrils flaring with that spicy scent she so adored and thought she'd never smell again.

"I was a fool, Caron. A complete fool. Jett had let me down, and I was taken off guard when I heard about you talking to the FBI."

"I didn't—"

He touched her lips with his fingers, and shivers raced down her spine with the intimate connection. "I know. You don't have to say another word except that you forgive me. I know we haven't known each other that long, but I know you're the one for me. I love you, Caron. I love you so much. Spend Christmas with me. Spend a lifetime with me."

"I love you, too," she said, tears spilling from her eyes as he hugged her and then kissed her—a long, loving kiss that promised passion would come later.

IT WAS THE DAY AFTER Christmas when Caron finally had the opportunity to give Baxter the Christmas present she'd considered and reconsidered. Standing in Baxter's bathroom—soon to be hers since she was moving in with him—she surveyed her red dress and the now infamous blond wig, with jitters in her stomach and a smile on her ruby-red lips. With a little thrill, she glanced at the emerald-cut white diamond sparkling on her finger. It had been her surprise Christmas gift.

She couldn't wait to see what he thought of her plan to seduce him Marilyn-style, and for once, she didn't think it was the bombshell, but Caron—that turned him on. She knew Baxter desired her, and that they could play a few bedroom games, without her feeling insecure. And *that* turned her on. She adored the idea of such freedom. Just as she adored Baxter.

He'd been wonderful with her grandmother, who had surprised Caron by unveiling officially her own romance, just as Caron had suspected. And time spent with Baxter's family had only proven them more likable than ever. But now, home with Baxter, ready to celebrate alone—that was what she'd been waiting for.

Caron turned on the stereo built into the wall and popped in the CD. The music started and she opened the door to the bedroom and posed in the doorway. Baxter lay on the bed eagerly awaiting her surprise. With confidence she never thought possible, Caron began her sexy striptease to the music, "Santa Baby." A striptease that ended with the most passionate, wonderful lovemaking of her life.

Hours later, wrapped in Baxter's strong, protective arms, she twined her fingers in the dark, sexy hair on his chest. "I think I should send the wig back."

He lifted his head. "I like the wig."

She grinned. "Oh, I know. So do I. But what if I'm

keeping some other girl from having the night of her life? I know I would never have wanted to miss mine."

"Send it back, then," he said, tightening his arms around her. "And I can only hope it turns out as lucky for the next guy as it did for me."

# _Epilogue_

IT WAS NEW YEAR'S EVE and Josie stood behind the costume shop's counter, with her boss nearby, pressing her to stay longer than she'd wished. She was eager to get home and get ready for her night out with Tom.

She was busy adding the day's receipts when the door jingled and opened. To her happy surprise, Tom walked through the door, a package in his hand.

"Last delivery of the night," he said, winking as Josie's boss turned away. "Headed home to get ready for my hot date."

Josie grinned and waved as he left, wondering if the package was one of his "special deliveries." They'd been blissfully dating for over a month, and he often brought her packages. Flowers. Chocolates. Sexy lingerie. Seemed he preferred her costumes to be of the tiny silk and satin variety, and Josie was having fun experimenting with what turned him from hot to hottest.

With eagerness, Josie ripped open the package and found the blond Marilyn wig. "What in the world?" She flipped open the enclosed card and read,

I considered keeping this, but decided not to be selfish. My night in the Marilyn costume turned into a lifetime of fantasy. Please make sure some other girl gets the same chance. Caron Avery.

Josie smiled, thinking about just how wonderful her night in the Marilyn costume had turned out, as well, when she noticed the red envelope she hadn't seen at first. She bit her lip, a fizzle of excitement darting through her, certain it was from Tom. She slipped open the seal and pulled out the heart-covered card. Inside read,

My New Year's resolution is to spend every New Year with you, Josie. Forever.

Joy filled Josie. Happy New Year, indeed. And to all, a silk and satin good-night.

She was quite certain it would be for her.

'THIS EVENING I'm flying to New York for two weeks,'
Jasim imparted with a casualness that made her heart sink
like a stone. 'That's why I had you brought here. I own this
apartment and you'll be comfortable here while I'm abroad.'

'I can afford my own accommodation although I may not
need it for long. I'll have another job by the time you
get back—'

Jasim released a slightly harsh laugh. 'There's no need for
you to look for another position. How would I ever see you?
Don't you understand what I'm offering you?'

Elinor stood very still. 'No, I must be incredibly thick
because I haven't quite worked out yet what you're offering
me….'

His charismatic smile slashed his lean dark visage.
'Naturally, I want to take care of you….'

'No, thanks.' Elinor forced a smile and mentally willed him not to demean her with some sordid proposition. 'The only man who will ever take *care* of me with my agreement will be my husband. I'm willing to wait for you to come back but I'm not willing to be kept by you. I'm a very independent woman and what I give, I give freely.'

Jasim frowned. 'You make it all sound so serious.'

'What happened between us last night left pure chaos in its wake. Right now, I don't know whether I'm on my head or my heels. I'll stay for a while because I have nowhere else to go in the short term. So maybe it's good that you'll be away for a while.'

Jasim pulled out his wallet to extract a card. 'My private number,' he told her, presenting her with it as though it was a precious gift, which indeed it was. Many women would have done just about anything to gain access to that direct hotline to him, but his staff guarded his privacy with scrupulous care.

Before he could close the wallet, his blood ran cold in his veins. How could he have made such a serious oversight? What if he had got her pregnant? He knew that an unplanned pregnancy would engulf his life like an avalanche, crush his freedom and suffocate him. He barely stilled a shudder at the threat of such an outcome and thought how ironic it was that what his older brother had longed and prayed for to secure the line to the throne should strike Jasim as an absolute disaster....

* * *

*What will proud Prince Jasim do if Elinor is expecting his royal baby? Perhaps an arranged marriage is the only solution! But will Elinor agree? Find out in DESERT PRINCE, BRIDE OF INNOCENCE by Lynne Graham [#2884], available from Harlequin Presents® in January 2010.*

Bestselling Harlequin Presents author

# Lynne Graham

brings you an exciting new miniseries:

## PREGNANT BRIDES

*Inexperienced and expecting, they're forced to marry*

Collect them all:

### DESERT PRINCE, BRIDE OF INNOCENCE

*January 2010*

### RUTHLESS MAGNATE, CONVENIENT WIFE

*February 2010*

### GREEK TYCOON, INEXPERIENCED MISTRESS

*March 2010*

# REQUEST YOUR FREE BOOKS!

## 2 FREE NOVELS PLUS 2 FREE GIFTS!

HARLEQUIN®

*Blaze*™

**Red-hot reads!**

**YES!** Please send me 2 FREE Harlequin® Blaze™ novels and my 2 FREE gifts (gifts are worth about $10). After receiving them, if I don't wish to receive any more books, I can return the shipping statement marked "cancel". If I don't cancel, I will receive 6 brand-new novels every month and be billed just $4.24 per book in the U.S. or $4.71 per book in Canada. That's a savings of 15% off the cover price. It's quite a bargain. Shipping and handling is just 50¢ per book.* I understand that accepting the 2 free books and gifts places me under no obligation to buy anything. I can always return a shipment and cancel at any time. Even if I never buy another book, the two free books and gifts are mine to keep forever.

151 HDN EYS2  351 HDN EYTE

| | | |
|---|---|---|
| Name | (PLEASE PRINT) | |
| Address | | Apt. # |
| City | State/Prov. | Zip/Postal Code |

Signature (if under 18, a parent or guardian must sign)

### Mail to the Harlequin Reader Service:
**IN U.S.A.:** P.O. Box 1867, Buffalo, NY 14240-1867
**IN CANADA:** P.O. Box 609, Fort Erie, Ontario L2A 5X3

Not valid to current subscribers of Harlequin Blaze books.

**Want to try two free books from another line?
Call 1-800-873-8635 or visit www.morefreebooks.com.**

\* Terms and prices subject to change without notice. Prices do not include applicable taxes. N.Y. residents add applicable sales tax. Canadian residents will be charged applicable provincial taxes and GST. Offer not valid in Quebec. This offer is limited to one order per household. All orders subject to approval. Credit or debit balances in a customer's account(s) may be offset by any other outstanding balance owed by or to the customer. Please allow 4 to 6 weeks for delivery. Offer available while quantities last.

**Your Privacy:** Harlequin Books is committed to protecting your privacy. Our Privacy Policy is available online at www.eHarlequin.com or upon request from the Reader Service. From time to time we make our lists of customers available to reputable third parties who may have a product or service of interest to you. If you would prefer we not share your name and address, please check here. ☐

HB09R3

## New Year, New Man!

*For the perfect New Year's punch,*
*blend the following:*

- *One woman determined to find her inner vixen*
- *A notorious—and notoriously hot!—playboy*
- *A provocative New Year's Eve bash*
- *An impulsive kiss that leads to a night of*
  *explosive passion!*

When the clock hits midnight Claire Daniels
kisses the guy standing closest to her, but
the kiss doesn't end after the bells stop ringing....

### Look for

# Moonstruck

### by *USA TODAY* bestselling author

# JULIE KENNER

*Available January*

---

## red-hot reads

www.eHarlequin.com

HB79518

# COMING NEXT MONTH

## Available December 29, 2009

**#513 BLAZING BEDTIME STORIES, VOLUME III  Tori Carrington and Tawny Weber**
*Bedtime Stories*
What better way to spend an evening than cuddling up with your better half, indulging in supersexy fairy tales? We guarantee that sleeping will be the last thing on your mind!

**#514 MOONSTRUCK  Julie Kenner**
Claire Daniels is determined to get her old boyfriend back. She's tired of being manless, especially during the holidays, and she'd like nothing more than a New Year's Eve kiss to start the year off right. And she gets just that. Too bad it's not her ex-boyfriend she's kissing…

**#515 MIDNIGHT RESOLUTIONS  Kathleen O'Reilly**
*Where You Least Expect It*
A sudden, special kiss between two strangers in Times Square on New Year's Eve turns unforgettable, and soon Rose Hildebrande and Ian Cumberland's sexy affair is smokin' hot despite the frosty weather. Will things cool off, though, once the holiday season ends?

**#516 SEXY MS. TAKES  Jo Leigh**
*Encounters*
It's New Year's Eve in Manhattan and the ball is about to drop in Times Square…. Bella, Willow and Maggie are on their way to the same blockbuster Broadway audition until fate—and three very sexy men—sideline their journey with sizzling results!

**#517 HER SECRET FLING  Sarah Mayberry**
Don't dip your pen in the office ink. Good advice for rookie columnist Poppy Birmingham. Too bad coworker Jake Stevens isn't listening. Their recent road trip has turned things from antagonistic to hedonistic! He wants to keep this fling on the down-low…but with heat this intense, that's almost impossible.

**#518 HIS FINAL SEDUCTION  Lori Wilde**
Signing up for an erotic fantasy vacation was Jorgina Gerard's ticket to reinventing herself. The staid accountant was more than ready for a change, but has she taken on too much when she meets and seduces the hot, very gorgeous every-woman-would-want-him Quint Mason? She's looking forward to finding out!

HBCNMBPA1209